MISSING YOU

LORI BELL

This book is a work of fiction. Names, characters, places and incidents are the product of the author's imagination or are used fictitiously. Any resemblance to actual events, locales, or persons, living or dead, is coincidental.

Copyright © 2015 by Lori Bell

All rights reserved. This book or any portion thereof may not be reproduced or used in any manner whatsoever without the express written permission of the publisher except for the use of brief quotations in a book review.

Cover photograph by CanStockPhoto

http://career-advice.monster.com/job-search/Company-Industry-Research/Seasonal-Process-in-Retail/article.aspx
http://www.polimoda.com/en/courses/masters/fashion-buying-product-management.html?gclid=CNy9wsCu4McCFYY9gQodjAoI4w
http://www.wisegeek.org/what-does-a-fashion-buyer-do.htm
https://en.wikipedia.org/wiki/Car_bomb
http://www.medicinenet.com/script/main/art.asp?articlekey=24572
http://orthopedics.about.com/cs/herniateddisk/a/ruptureddisk_2.htm?utm_term=treatment%20for%20herniated%20discs&utm_content=p1-main-1-title&utm_medium=sem&utm_source=msn&utm_ campaign=adid-f18e803e-5dfc-412f-9c12-e9e58a93b490-0-ab_msb_ocode-28794&ad= semD&an =msn_s&am =broad&q= treatment%20 for%20herniated%20discs &dqi=&o=28794&l =sem&qsrc =999&askid=f18e803e-5dfc-412f-9c12-e9e58a93b490-0-ab_msbhttp://www.healio.com/cardiology/stroke/news/online /%7B4d9054c0-bd6c-4af6-be8d-9158858e16fc%7D/what-is-a-stroke?gclid=CKTVg9qep8gCFZQdgQod83UPHw

Printed by CreateSpace

ISBN 978-1517767532

DEDICATION

To my dear friend, Judy Ottensmeier:
I'm not sure there was anyone else on this earth who was more excited to read and promote every single one of my books. You were so proud to call me your friend and to tell everyone I was an author. I miss your love, your encouragement, and simply having you exist in my life. The night you left this earth, my heart broke. I'm both sad and proud to dedicate my seventh release to you. Missing You was ironically written and titled before I had any inclination that I truly would be missing you.

February 20, 1957 – October 11, 2015

CHAPTER 1

Brooke Carey swiftly closed the door to her cabin. The minus twenty-five degree wind chill had easily gone right through her body as she trekked from her midsized, all-wheel drive sport utility vehicle and up two steps to the front porch leading into her log cabin. The soles of her boots were snow packed, and she planted her feet square in the middle of the inside mat and bent forward to pull them off. The rug was wet where she stood now and she could feel her socks soaking up the cold snow which wasn't too quick to melt. It was cold in that twelve-hundred-square-foot cabin. Brooke had been gone for hours. The fire in the fireplace was long out and the furnace was set to run at sixty-eight degrees. She left her wet boots directly in front of the door and walked through the living room, removing her white down parka and throwing it over the back of the red sectional. Winters in Breckenridge, Colorado could be brutal.

She turned no lights on until she reached her bedroom. Moments later, her dark-washed skinny jeans and thick, white cowl neck sweater lay on a pile on the dark hardwood floor near her bed. Only wearing the top half of long-sleeved pink flannel pajamas, with a pair of fluffy heather-gray socks, Brooke pulled the covers back and quickly slipped into bed in an effort to warm up.

It had been a pleasant evening. Dinner with her two closest friends always left Brooke feeling refreshed, and loved. Their stories were never dull and their time spent catching up over food and alcohol was something the three of them have been doing at least quarterly since they graduated high school ten years prior. No matter how busy their lives became, they swore to never lose touch. And they hadn't.

Tia Kenney was the diva in their bunch. Her long hair was highlighted blonde, and to those she met in the last decade, she never admitted to not having a natural hair color. She didn't have to, because she never allowed a single root to show. Her five-eight frame was curvy, toned and virtually perfect. Tia owned a salon, located downtown, scenic Breckenridge. Following cosmetology school, Tia launched her own business and quickly found success in hairstyling, nail care, makeup, and skincare. She now had experienced staff working for her at *Illusions by TK*, because a business venture which sent her in another direction two years ago had paid off in spades when Tia created *Reality*, her own skincare line. Her looks, her incredible business success, and her eight-year marriage to a physical therapist made any woman envious. But not Brooke. Brooke had always seen past the flawless facade and perfect life, as she's loved Tia through thick and thin.

It was their mutual friend, Mollie Sawyer who could be judgy. She didn't think Tia would be happy in her marriage, raising another woman's child. Tia never wanted to have children, but when she met Bo Kenney, he had already had a baby of his own. Bo was a packaged deal with Baby Mac. He didn't have a mother, and Tia quickly fell for both him and his father. Mac, now eight years old, continues to be the brightest light in Tia's life. She's the only mother he's ever known, and she has worn her heart on her sleeve for him since the day she met him. She would give up her own life for that boy. He was hers.

But, Mollie, five-foot-five with a stocky frame, who birthed four children in eight years, two boys and two girls, never understood Tia's way of thinking. *How could she not want a baby of her own flesh and blood? How could she marry a man who already came with baggage?* Mollie, also twenty-eight years old like her friends, Brooke and Tia, was far more old school. She was a virgin until after marriage, unlike both of her friends. She gave up her two-year registered nursing degree to become a stay-at-home mom. Fortunately for Mollie, her husband Freddy was an orthopedic surgeon and they could afford the luxury of only having one household income.

Brooke wasn't swimming in money like her friends were. She was content with the success she had found being a retail buyer. She was good at planning and selecting clothing and accessories to sell in retail outlets. She was a natural at considering customer demand, price, quality and availability. Her job required time spent in her Breckenridge office as well as frequent travel in order to assemble new collections of merchandise. Over the past six months however, Brooke had become a recluse. She worked from her cabin. She did attend weekly meetings at her downtown office. But, travel had been out of the question for awhile. Her boss and her clients understood, and they were just giving her the time she needed.

It was difficult for Brooke to be with her girlfriends tonight. They have forced her to meet them twice now when she didn't feel up to it, but joined them anyway. They never noticed how she pushed her food around on her plate, eventually covering most of it with her napkin. They didn't appear to pay any attention to the glasses of Cabernet she asked the waitress to bring, one after another. Or maybe they did notice. Maybe they just wanted her to feel better. *Don't eat if you're not hungry. Have another drink if that's what you want, or feel like you need. Just do what you have to do to find your old self again.*

Brooke turned on her side in her king-sized bed, sliding one arm underneath her pillow to force her head upright. She looked toward her nightstand, where she still had a lamp lit. It had become a ritual for her. Every night, before bed, she stared at his photograph. It was her favorite picture of him, standing outside of the cabin. It was early spring then as some of the snow was beginning to melt. He looked dapper, wearing his dark-washed denim, black turtleneck sweater, and charcoal gray hiking boots. His jet-black hair was combed perfectly on his head. Never a hair out of place on that man. He liked everything to be *just so*. It was one of his quirks, but Brooke loved that about him, too.

Brooke wanted to talk to his photograph, but she had run out of words. The tears were mostly all gone now as well. It didn't make any sense. People do not just vanish. She loved him for two years. They shared everything, even the bed she was alone in now. They were supposed to share their lives together. But, just like that, they were no longer together. Because he was gone.

CHAPTER 2

After four hours of restless sleep, Brooke got out of bed, tied her long dark hair up in a messy knot on top of her head, and grabbed her white fleece robe spread out on the foot end of the bed as she made her way to the kitchen to start a pot of coffee. Coffee and wine were what she had lived on for the past year. She had lost weight and it was evident on her five-six-and-a-half size eight frame which was closer to a size four now. She looked too thin, she recognized, but that's what something crazy happening had done to her. She had no desire to eat. She could barely find the will to breathe.

When she poured her first cup of coffee, it was steaming in front of her as she sat down at the table. She was thinking about the conversation she had with Tia at the restaurant last night after Mollie had gone home. It wasn't unusual for the two of them to have one more drink after Mollie was called home early to tend to one of her children. Sometimes she made the choice to call it a night because she was tired from caring for four small children.

Earlier in the evening, the three of them had talked about how it had been twelve months since Bryce Lanning had gone missing. Brooke admitted to them both how it still seemed surreal and the struggle to live day-to-day suffocated her at times. But, she also put up a good front and told them she would be okay, one moment at a time.

"So how are you really doing?" Tia asked Brooke when it was just the two of them with refilled glasses of Cabernet.

"You didn't believe my one-moment-at-a-time spiel?" Brooke asked from behind her tipped wine glass.

"I think saying it, saying you will be okay, is a good start." Tia continued to worry about her dearest friend. She didn't look well. Tia was all about looking fit and fabulous, but Brooke's transformation to thin was unhealthy. She almost looked frail, and her eyes bore sadness and pain.

"Bryce is out there somewhere, T," Brooke spoke, softly. "I need to know what happened and why and where. How in the hell am I supposed to carry on with so many unanswered questions? I still expect him to walk through the door. I check my phone hourly to see if he's tried to contact me." Brooke would only admit that to Tia. Had Mollie known, she would tell her Bryce wasn't worth missing. She never did like him, or ever believed he was deserving of her best friend.

"I understand," Tia began. "I can't imagine the feelings racing through your mind and body, but I hurt for you, just seeing you dredge through this."

"Thank you," Brooke responded, touching Tia's hand on top of the table.

"But," Tia added, "it's time to start taking better care of yourself. Time to begin to let go, and maybe even open up to the fact that you may never know."

***

ONE YEAR AGO

It took an hour for Brooke to make it home. The snowstorm was one of the worst Breckenridge had seen in several years. They already had three feet of snow on the ground and just as much was expected through the night. It was something Brooke was used to, but she still always felt relieved to make it to her cabin and know she would be in for the night. She assumed Bryce was on his way home, too.

An hour passed. The cabin was cozy with the fireplace glowing and it smelled delicious to Brooke in the kitchen as she simmered bulk pork sausage in thick, white gravy on the stovetop and readied to put homemade biscuits in the oven. Breakfast for dinner was one of Bryce's favorites, and Brooke had grown to love it as well. That was all they were having for dinner. No sides. Just a tall glass of milk, over ice, for Bryce and a hot cup of black coffee for Brooke. She drank that stuff all day long most days.

Another thirty minutes had passed before Brooke was tired of standing in the kitchen and began to wonder about Bryce. She knew the weather had to be keeping him, and she texted his phone to check on him. He never responded. It wasn't unlike him not to respond immediately, but Brooke had hoped he would give her peace of mind that he was on his way home.

She turned off the stovetop burner and then the wall oven. The biscuits sat raw on a tray on the counter. The gravy was bubbling under a lid in the deep skillet. The coffee was getting cold. Brooke was worried, but she also felt angry at Bryce for not alerting her to where he was and why he was late. *Was he still at work? Was he in trouble in this treacherous weather?* It was almost seven o'clock and already completely dark.

She had tried calling Bryce three times by nine o'clock and then the next call she made was to his brother. Blain Lanning was three years younger than Bryce at thirty-one, and a completely opposite type of man. Bryce was tall, six-foot-two, with thick jet-black hair and gorgeous chiseled features. Blain was shorter, at five-foot-nine, with light brown, almost dishwater blond, hair. His facial features weren't as dashing as his elder brother's because he looked more boyish. He had a mischievous grin with dimples that added to his naughty charm. Bryce was the businessman. Blain was the playboy. Blain worked for the City of Breckenridge, and he worked hard. But, he also lived to punch the time clock at the end of the day and go play. Not many women could resist a man like Blain, and he knew it. He and Bryce were not close, but they were brothers and that was why Brooke reached out to him that night.

It took him half the time it would have taken anyone else to get to the cabin in what the weather channel was calling the *blizzard of the decade* for parts of Colorado. Brooke could hear the city's snow plow coming from a half a mile away as Blain made his way to the cabin. She was waiting for him outside the door when he walked up. His trademark was to wear tight, faded denim and a flannel shirt with tan hiking boots, laced up to the middle of his calves.

"Not here yet, huh?" Blain asked her as she stepped back to invite him inside. She was wearing fitted, black yoga pants with flared bottoms and an oversized lilac fleece hoodie. She had shoved her feet in her calf-high charcoal gray sheepskin boots to meet him on the snow-covered porch. She slipped out of those boots and left them by the door when they went inside. Blain remained standing on the mat in front of the door in his own snow-covered, wet boots.

Brooke shook her head in response, "I wish he would at least call me."

The weather worsened after Brooke invited Blain to shed his boots and sit down on the red sectional in the living room, near the fire. He was supposed to be out working, plowing the streets for the third time today, but at the rate the snow was coming down, there was no use. Waiting it out inside of his truck or staying with Brooke was the same difference. And he preferred not to leave Brooke alone, because he could see how worried she was about his brother. He was beginning to be as well.

"Have things been okay between the two of you?" Blain dared to ask. He didn't know her all that well, but after two years of dating his brother, he considered her a part of the family. And he knew his parents, who also lived in Breckenridge, cared about her.

"What? Oh, yeah, we're good. We've always been good." That wasn't an entirely truthful answer, Brooke knew, but what couples didn't have their trials? Blain nodded his head, in acceptance.

"So I'm sure it's just this blizzard mess and maybe he doesn't have reception for his phone," Blain explained. "There have been a few power outages reported." Talking to him had already made Brooke feel at ease. Things like this happened. Maybe she should not have panicked and called Blain.

After an hour and a half passed with Blain going in and out of the cabin to check the weather as well as having phone conversations with his coworkers stationed in plows throughout the city, Brooke offered to put the biscuits in the oven and reheat the gravy. Blain told her he was hungry, but not to go through any trouble.

Brooke sipped a cup of coffee while she watched Blain eat a heaping plate of breakfast food at a few minutes before midnight. "It is technically morning at almost midnight, so breakfast works for me," Blain said, putting a generous forkful into his mouth. Brooke smiled at him. He had a hefty appetite. He could out-eat his brother, for sure, but Bryce was always counting calories. He splurged on things, like biscuits and gravy, but punished himself the following day at the gym. Both brothers were fit and had inherited good genes, for sure.

The weather conditions forced Blain to stay put all night. They were obviously snowed-in as the path to Brooke's mid-sized SUV was blanketed with a foot of snow. Blain told her he would clear it all, including her lane, with his plow in the morning. Then he agreed to allow her to go along with him in the plow to downtown Breckenridge. They were both convinced that Bryce had stayed the night at his office, and possibly had no cell service. Still, no matter how much Brooke tried to conceal her worry, Blain could see it in her eyes and hear it in her voice. His only wish now was for his big brother to have a damn good excuse for making a woman like Brooke worry about him.

At daybreak, Brooke suited up in jeans, a heavy yellow sweater and her black snowsuit over top. She went outside to find Blain had already cleared a drivable path and was working on uncovering her vehicle. "That can wait," she told him. "Let's go into town with the plow." He knew she meant it was time to find Bryce. She couldn't wait any longer.

Just as the two of them were buckling up inside of his plow truck, another one was headed down the narrow lane leading to where they were parked near the cabin. Blain immediately opened his driver's side door and stepped out into the snow, and when Brooke saw a police officer get out of the passenger side of the other truck, she hurried to get out.

As both Blain and Brooke approached the officer, Blain spoke first. "Clarke! Nice weather we're having. What brings you out here?" Blain momentarily held his breath, trying not to assume the worst case scenario.

Detective Ty Clarke looked at Brooke before speaking. And when he finally spoke, Brooke no longer felt the cold wind chill in her face. A numbness overtook her. "Miss Carey, we found Mr. Lanning's truck about five miles from here, alongside the roadway. We found it a few hours ago when we were first able to get out and moving once the storm passed."

"And Bryce? He's around too, right?" Blain abruptly interrupted.

"No sir," the police officer responded. "He has not turned up yet. The door to his truck was wide open on the driver's side. It appeared he ran out of gas. His cell phone and wallet were both found on the seat. There were no prints or tracks of any kind in the snow as we were dumped on all night long. We do have a few men on the lookout, searching the area where the truck was left."

The only words Brooke could put together were, "Oh my God!" as Blain grabbed her hard around the shoulders overtop of her down parka. "We'll find him. Come on, in my truck, we'll help search."

Blain didn't want to ask Ty Clarke, a trusted officer of the law, any further questions in front of Brooke. He just wanted to push through the snow-packed roads, form his own tunnel if he had to, and get to his brother. Wherever he was.

***

Brooke finished her coffee and stood up from the table. It had been one year already. Last weekend had marked the twelve-month anniversary date of when Bryce had gone missing. There wasn't half as much snow on the ground right now, as Thanksgiving was approaching. In ten days, Brooke would be forced to muddle through yet another holiday. She was sad to be alone most of the time, and sick and tired of the worry which consumed her and felt more like grief most days. She didn't believe that Bryce was dead. She hadn't allowed herself to accept that. And wouldn't. At least not unless she was forced to, and there had been no proof. Not a single lead or clue to explain Bryce's disappearance.

She stood up from the table and noticed her coffee cup had left a ring. She didn't think twice before walking over to the sink to dampen a dish cloth under the faucet. Then, she stopped. She just stood there, alone in her kitchen, thinking how she really didn't care if there was a coffee stained ring on the tabletop. It was Bryce who was anal about every mess being cleaned up. He used to get angry about the littlest things.

Brooke placed the dish cloth back in the sink, and she walked out of the kitchen, leaving the stain to dry on the tabletop.

CHAPTER 3

Brooke worked the entire morning on her laptop at a desk in her bedroom. She was still wearing her pink flannel pajamas, both top and bottom, with no socks, as she checked the retail sales figures in the stores she was in charge of. Winter wear had been stocked in the stores since late September. To be successful in this industry, Brooke was accustomed to planning her products and marketing approaches months in advance. Six months ago, she was finished with winter wear. She almost wished she was busier this time of the year. She planned to attend the trade shows early next year, in both January and February, but getting through the holidays again would be difficult.

She closed out of her laptop at noon, feeling pleased with the budget and the sales figures. Christmas shoppers in the next four weeks were sure to make it an even more successful winter season for the buyers in her Colorado firm. Brooke was going to break for lunch and then resume working. Her focus the rest of the day was going to be on the supply chain, as she strived to lower the risk each season of running out of high-demand stock.

Brooke's job fueled her on most days. She didn't just feel productive, she felt valuable, and that was something she desperately desired in her life in the past year since Bryce disappeared. She slipped off her pajamas and left them in a pile on the hardwood floor next to her bed. She walked naked through her bedroom and out into the hallway toward the bathroom. She turned on the light and then the shower water. While she waited for it to heat up, she caught her reflection in the mirror. She had lost weight. Considerable weight. Her curves were gone, and she didn't recognize the bone thin woman staring back at her in the mirror hanging above the vanity. She used to feel very comfortable with her body. She used to take care of it, and it showed.

After her shower, Brooke blow-dried her long, dark hair and pulled it up into a high ponytail and then she applied some light makeup to her face. She dressed in skinny dark-washed jeans, a chunky pale pink sweater and high dark brown boots. While she was taking a shower, she had decided today she would not live on another pot of coffee. She was going out, to the grocery store, and she would stock her refrigerator with food. Some days she felt more empowered than others. She was suddenly feeling like today was going to be a good day.

An hour later, she had four paper bags in her cart as she pushed it through the grocery store's parking lot. It was only eleven degrees, but the wind was still and Brooke found it refreshing to be outside. She was bundled in her white down parka again with gloves to match, and she had almost reached the back end of her black SUV when she heard someone call out to her. And then she turned to find Blain walking up.

"I hope those groceries mean you're cooking Thanksgiving dinner," Blain said, wondering if he should have brought it up. He knew she hated the holidays now, without Bryce. But, it was an inside joke between the two of them. His and Bryce's mother was not the best cook in Breckenridge, yet they've eaten her food together many times in an effort to not hurt her feelings. Bryce used to complain outright at the dinner table, refusing to eat a few times. Blain hated when his mother was upset, he often times wanted to knock his brother out.

"Just admit you love my cooking, go on, I'm not shy, I welcome the compliments," Brooke said, smiling at him. He too was bundled in the cold weather. Under his tan, hooded Carhartt coat, she could see another flannel shirt peeking out.

"Best damn cook ever, but don't tell my mother I said that," Blain replied, returning her smile. He hadn't seen her in well over a month. He had made a point to call or stop by the cabin every few weeks or so to check on her, or just to catch up. They often times compared notes with the last time they consulted with the Breckenridge Police Department. There were never any new leads. They both feared the case was closed, and they were just not being told.

"Will you be there on Thanksgiving?" Brooke asked, knowing Blain would be. He was the only son his parents had left now. *Until Bryce comes back.* The reality, the unlikely chance of that ever truly happening, was beginning to sink in Brooke's mind. She just couldn't bring herself to allow her heart to heal.

"Yes," he answered, "and please tell me you will be, too." She could see Blain's breath in the cold as they stood only a few feet apart.

"I was hoping to drum up a good excuse," she admitted.

"Just go, it'll make you feel better to be around people on the holiday. Won't it?" he asked, wondering if he couldn't be more wrong. Maybe being with Bryce's family made her pain worse.

"A holiday is just another day to me anymore," she responded, not wanting to tell him seeing his parents always made her miss Bryce so much more. There was constant hurt in his mother's eyes, and his father was an older, carbon copy of Bryce. "Besides, I couldn't care less to see you show up with another whore on your arm."

Blain laughed loud and deep, from the pit of his stomach. They both knew better. His sex life, his women, were kept completely separate from his parents. He never brought any woman home to meet his mother and father. He was never that serious about any of them. He was all about having fun, and never fathomed settling down. His laugh was contagious and Brooke chimed in with him. Then, he said, "It's just going to be you and me against mom and dad. Don't leave me hanging, lady."

"I'll be there. I'll call your mother this week to see if there is anything I can bring," she told him.

"Oh please offer to bring the turkey or the dressing, something delicious and heavy to fill my belly for the day." Brooke laughed at him as he told her goodbye, and he would see her soon.

After Brooke made it back to the cabin, she carried her grocery bags inside and unpacked. She had bought the ingredients for a cheeseburger potato soup that her grandmother used to make for her when she was a little girl. The recipe was a favorite in their family. Brooke missed her family, but she never went home anymore. She wasn't even sure where home was. She grew up in Colorado, first in Denver and then she and her parents moved to Breckenridge when she was a teenager. Her parents divorced when she was a sophomore in high school, and her father remarried a woman half his age. He even had a baby girl with her. There was no room for Brooke in his life after he started a second family. His young wife made sure of that. And then her father's wife convinced him to move to Florida. Brooke's mother was a retired grade school music teacher and she found her mature friends far more exciting than her family. She now lived in Fairfax, Virginia. She played bridge, sang in the church choir, and traveled. Brooke always found it funny how her mother's frequent flyer miles were never used to come out west to visit her. They probably saw each other once a year, if that. She had not come to visit Brooke, or reached out with more than a phone call after her life was in crisis when Bryce disappeared. Her mother had only met Bryce once, and the two of them hadn't thought too much of each other. Bryce's parents, moreso his mother, had actually felt more like family to Brooke than she admitted, and she did want to see them over the holidays. *Maybe it will be easier this year,* she told herself.

The soup was simmering on the stovetop when Brooke made her way back into her bedroom, and sat down on her desk chair to power on her laptop. She wanted to get a couple more hours of work in today. She had to research the supply chain, and make more budget notes. She expected the numbers to be good, better than last year. She was always striving to outdo previous quotas. In her career, she wanted to continue to learn and be better. In her personal life, she never felt that way. When she met Bryce, she believed he was the one. He completed her and she loved him. She wanted to spend the rest of her life with him. They had talked about marriage, and Bryce never wavered. They had lived together for eighteen months. Only six months after they met, Bryce already moved into the cabin with Brooke. Her cabin was bigger than the loft apartment he had been renting in downtown Breckenridge. Now, Blain was renting one of those lofts.

Brooke sat in front of her computer, only staring at the log-in screen. Despite their differences, Bryce Lanning was the one for her. He wasn't the most romantic man in the world, but he could be kind and gentle and his desire to delve into his career as an accountant was attractive to her. He wanted to be successful, and he wanted to have someone to share his life with. He wasn't spontaneous or adventurous, but he offered stability for Brooke. He didn't apologize with words when he was wrong, but he knew how to wrap her up in his arms without speaking and hold her with a tenderness that made her cave each and every time. She missed being held in his arms, and since she now had allowed her mind to go there, to think about the good in that man, she missed him more than ever. And she had just made this potentially good day another sad one.

Distracting herself with work, witnessing the incredible, climbing sales figures on her computer screen did make her feel better after awhile. And two hours later, she logged off her computer and went into the kitchen to eat a bowl of soup. She enjoyed it. It tasted good to her and she ate the entire bowl. When she was finished, she put some of it in the refrigerator to eat again in the coming days, and then she realized she had made entirely too much. She filled a second, large bowl with the remaining soup and instead of freezing it, she picked up her cell phone and called Tia. She answered on the second ring.

"Hey," she spoke into the phone and Brooke smiled at the sound of her voice. Tia was a woman who had her own skincare line and could easily call herself a millionaire. But, to Brooke, she was just T. And her *hey* greeting on the other end of the phone was simply nice to hear.

"Hey yourself," Brooke spoke, and she sounded happy to Tia.

"Having a good day?" Tia asked, hoping so.

"Yes, making it a good day, I guess you could say."

"That's my girl. So, what's going on? Wine hangover gone and you need me again?" Tia smiled into the phone as she spoke.

Brooke laughed before she responded. "This will sound silly, but I cooked a pot of soup today. I don't know, I saw myself in the mirror and realized I'm going to wrinkle and wither away if I don't start taking better care of myself. Anyway, I went overboard with the amount of cheeseburger potato soup I made and I'm wondering if you all would like some."

"While I'm glad to hear that you are slowly coming back to life, I'm going to decline the soup. You obviously have forgotten that the mere thought of potatoes makes me throw up in my mouth," Tia laughed, but she wasn't joking.

"You're a mess," Brooke said with a broad smile on her face, sitting alone on the red sectional in her living room now. She had left the mess and the dishes behind in the kitchen. "I'll call Mollie. I'm sure her kids will eat anything."

"Just as long as they eat it and Mollie doesn't. She's a chunky monkey these days," Tia said, being unkind because she was the toned, thin one.

"Be nice, T! Mollie has four kids to keep up with every day. She doesn't have time for herself, and she's exhausted by the end of every day." Brooke meant her words, in defense of how hard Mollie strived to keep her children and her husband happy. And, the more she thought about it, she liked Tia's idea of offering the soup to Mollie. If she had already prepared dinner for tonight, she could serve the soup tomorrow. Maybe she would enjoy not having to cook a meal.

"I know, I know, I'm such a bitch sometimes," Tia said, attempting to sound regretful.

The two of them ended their phone conversation a few minutes later when Tia's son Mac needed to be picked up from indoor soccer practice. After Brooke ended their call, she decided to just deliver the soup, unannounced, to Mollie.

The Sawyer's house was five miles closer to town than Brooke's, but it was still located in the outskirts of Breckenridge. Brooke made the turn down their lane road and drove directly up to their house. It was beginning to get dark and she did notice light coming from the main level of their two-story, forty-five-hundred-square-foot home. It was immense, compared to what Brooke was used to, but with four kids Mollie always said they needed the space. It seemed like a good way to cover up how Freddy always wanted bigger and better, and, well, the best of everything.

A few minutes later, Brooke was standing on their front porch, holding the large, lidded bowl of soup in her gloved hands. And to her surprise, it was Freddy who answered the door. Brooke noticed how his brown hair was receding a bit at age thirty seven. He was still wearing what looked like his work clothes, black dress pants, white button-down shirt with a red print tie. Boring, but she could picture him wearing a white lab coat over it all and strutting his stuff up and down the hospital halls. Freddy Sawyer had an arrogance about him, and though she tried, Brooke never was able to warm up to him. His belly hung over his belt too much, and Brooke was thinking the last thing he needed was a bowl of potato soup, as she smiled what she hoped looked genuine and spoke first. "Hello Freddy. Nice to see you! Is Mollie home?"

"Of course she's home," he said awkwardly as if his wife belonged there, as if she was chained to the house around the clock. He did manage to step back for Brooke to enter the foyer, and when she stepped inside, she saw Mollie. Her long, auburn curls were messy on her head and pulled back into a low ponytail. She was wearing baggy pink sweat pants and a stained oversized white t-shirt. It looked as if one of her little ones had put his or her messy hands all over it.

"Brooke! What brings you here, honey?" Mollie asked, sounding and appearing overjoyed to see her.

"Soup," Brooke answered, feeling like she was doing something nice for her overworked and underappreciated friend. She looked spent and it was only quarter to six in the evening.

"You made it? For us?" Mollie asked, sounding surprised, because that just was not something Brooke did. Especially not in the last year. She had barely been taking care of herself, much less others.

"I made it for myself, it's my grandma's cheeseburger potato soup recipe, and I made too much. I'm here to share if you want some?" Brooke hadn't seen Mollie look so appreciative, and happy, in a long time. Maybe because no one had done anything for her in what seemed like ages.

"I remember when you made it once, and I would love to have that again! Dinner is already in the oven and almost ready for tonight, but you're saving me from slaving over the stove at least one evening this week. Thank you," Mollie said, hugging Brooke with the large bowl in the middle of them. By now, Freddy had slipped out of the room, thinking he had done so unnoticed, but Brooke noticed. And, this wasn't the first time she wondered what her dear friend ever saw in that man. Maybe it was different when they first met when Mollie was doing clinicals for her nursing degree in the same hospital where Freddy had already been working as an orthopedic surgeon for a few years. Still, Brooke and Tia had always agreed Freddy Sawyer was an arrogant SOB.

Their conversation was brief in the marbled-floor foyer as Mollie had to tend to fighting and crying coming from the kitchen. It was chaotic in their home, but Brooke enjoyed being there for a few minutes. It sure beat the deafening silence in her cabin.

CHAPTER 4

Brooke opened her eyes on Thanksgiving morning, and as soon as she did, she wished she could have closed them again. Holidays were a special time for family gatherings, sharing food, drinks, and moments with the people you loved. Without Bryce, it was not like that anymore for Brooke, and she wanted this day to pass just like any other. But, she had promised Bryce's mother she would be there, at their family dinner table, at one o'clock. She also agreed to bring a pumpkin pie so she needed to get out of bed, and prepare to bake.

She wanted to show up in yoga pants and an oversized sweatshirt. That's how she felt about making an effort to get herself ready. There were six inches of snow on the ground from overnight, so that helped her make the choice to just wear dark-washed skinny jeans, nearly knee high camel-colored boots, and a warm, also camel-colored sweater, to match. She felt better once she got dressed, and she left the cabin promptly at twelve-thirty. She knew it would take her exactly twenty minutes to get there and she, out of respect, didn't want to be late. Her father, if he ever taught her anything when she was growing up, believed arriving ten minutes early anywhere was simply courteous.

When she drove into the modest cul-de-sac, mostly consisting of condos and townhouses, Brooke suddenly felt like she couldn't breathe. It was as if she was going to have a panic attack, but she forced her mind right as she pulled into the driveway, shifted into park, and turned off the ignition. And then, right behind her, she saw a powder blue Hummer enter the drive. Blain was now there, too, and when he got out of his vehicle first, he walked up to hers and opened her driver's side door.

"I'll carry the turkey in for you," he teased and she smiled.

"Or rather, the pumpkin pie?" she asked him, getting out and nearly standing up to his height on the shoveled concrete in her two-and-half-inch high boots. They were warm, but not the most practical to wear out and about in the fresh-fallen snow.

"Holy Christ, I think you grew since the last time I saw you at the grocery store. Share with me what you've been eating, I need some," Blain was joking and she knew he was referring to how he was always the short brother. And, suddenly, she was missing Bryce, his tall frame, and everything else about him, again.

"They're just heels, you can try them on if you'd like," she teased, handing him the pie from the floor of the backseat, while struggling to pretend this day was a happy one for her.

"Oh? Nice. Maybe after this party?" They both giggled and walked up to the front door. Brooke waited for Blain to open it and walk in first. It was his parents' home. She would have rang the bell. Suddenly this was all too weird as she felt like she was showing up for Thanksgiving dinner with her missing boyfriend's playboy brother.

The day did get better as dinner was tasty, not delicious but good, and the company was as expected. Bill Lanning sat in front of the television in his recliner chair ninety percent of the time, except for during dinner. He was polite, but not overly talkative with any of them. Brooke caught herself staring at him a few times because he was an older version of Bryce. His father was sixty-one years old and Bryce was thirty-one when he went missing last year. Blain resembled his mother in looks. Julie Lanning was fifty-nine years old and the pain and worry she had been through in the last year had aged her considerably. She cried a few times throughout the day, and at one point when she and Brooke were alone in the kitchen, she grabbed her and clung to her and just sobbed. She, too, didn't want to believe anything terrible had happened to her son. But, after all this time, she had begun to not only fear the worst, but believe it.

✼✼✼

After playing two never-ending games of Rummikub at the kitchen table with both Julie and Blain, Brooke pretended to feel regretful about needing to get going home. She thanked Julie for inviting her and then Julie cried again. Brooke held her another time, but it was exhausting for her to be strong for someone else when all she wanted to do was continue to spiral further from the reality of this situation.

Blain recognized her pain, and he too said he needed to leave. He followed Brooke out to her car and took the opportunity to lift her spirits before she drove off and went home, alone. "You don't have to pretend anymore," he told her.

"What?" she asked him, before opening her driver's side door.

"It's over. Another holiday has come and gone. It's okay to say it sucks and you'd rather not do it again next year."

"And this is coming from you? The one who guilted me into joining him here today?" Brooke was partly teasing, but her words were true.

"Women tend to give in to me," he teased, and she saw his dimpled smile and couldn't help but grin at him.

"You're a spoiled baby," she said, opening her car to get inside.

"Have a drink with me downtown," he offered. "I think we both need it after tears and Rummikub all afternoon." Brooke glanced up at the house and then back at Blain.

"It's a holiday. Nothing's open except for Ruby's Bar on Sycamore Street," she said, seriously.

"My thoughts exactly, but how the hell do you know Ruby's hours?" Blain asked her.

"I've seen the inside of a bar room before," she answered.

"Before Bryce," he added, and for some reason, Brooke didn't feel as sad this time.

"It's okay that he didn't feel comfortable in bars," Brooke defended him.

"Sure it is," Blain said, appearing sincere. "That just forced you to have a stash of Cabernet at home instead."

"That sounds so good to me right now," she admitted.

"See, I told you. Let's go. I'll follow you to Ruby's for that Cab."

"I meant home, and my stash," she responded.

"I'm not letting you drink alone on a holiday. What kind of turkey would I be if I allowed that?" Brooke smiled at him, and then shook her head at him, while she replied. "Just one drink."

***

There were only three others in the bar when Blain followed Brooke to Ruby's. She sat down at a table for two against the far wall and Blain walked up to the bar, joining her a few minutes later with a bottle of Cabernet and two wine glasses.

"I thought I said just one," she reminded him.

"Yes, one bottle," he smiled as he sat down in his tight denim and green flannel shirt.

Brooke took a long sip and Blain watched her before she spoke. He was wondering something, and debating if he should ask her. It had been a year. She seemed to look better, maybe even feel better. His guess was she had finally started to accept what life had thrown at her.

"I went to the police station last week," she told him, and he raised his eyebrows as she continued. "I wanted them to add something to the flyer which is still posted all over town and beyond." Blain was thinking, after a year, *what could she possibly add to Bryce's missing information?* Everything pertinent was included already. The date he went missing, details of his physical appearance, and where to contact if he was seen. "He had a freckle on his left elbow. I had forgotten about that, and it's something they needed to know." It sounded utterly ridiculous and Blain felt sorry for her. He was just thinking, and hoping, she had finally accepted Bryce was not coming back. Now she had this crazy idea that a freckle could bring him home.

"On his elbow?" Blain asked.

"Yes," Brooke replied, totally oblivious to how ridiculous she sounded.

"Most of us are running around in this frigid part of the country with long sleeves on our shirts and multiple layers. Who in the Sam hell is able to even look at people's elbows?" Blain's tone sounded annoyed and Brooke immediately picked up on it.

"Well excuse me if I'm still grasping at the smallest things, yes something as trivial as a freckle." Brooke stopped making eye contact with Blain and she could feel her eyes welling up with tears. She took her time, one sip following another, and she finished the wine in her glass before either of them spoke again.

"It's okay. I'm sorry. I'm being insensitive. I just hoped you were beginning to let go. Eventually, you're going to have to accept that he's not coming back." Blain tried to say those words sincerely, but he had anger in his voice. He hated his brother for leaving them all with an unsolved mystery. He hated the pain he witnessed, time and again, in his mother's eyes, and most of all he couldn't bear to see Brooke heartbroken.

"I'm not sure I'll ever be able to fully let go," she admitted. "It's just not right to give up on someone you planned a life with."

"Had my brother ever proposed to you?" Blain asked, feeling like the alcohol was beginning to talk. He felt freer to ask her personal questions.

"No, but we just knew we wanted to spend our lives together." Brooke suddenly felt like she had to defend their relationship.

"What if he wanted out? What if he left on his own free will? You know, my father did that to my mother once. He just packed his things and left one day when Bryce and I were in grade school and my mother was out running errands or something. He was gone for six weeks. My mother made excuses, one right after another for that bastard. I don't even know why he came back, but I can still remember him waltzing in during dinner and sitting down and expecting us all to carry on as if nothing had happened. Bryce was always a lot like him. Selfish."

Brooke didn't know what to say. She knew Bill Lanning was not the warm and fuzzy type, but she had no idea he was capable of walking out on his family. "Bryce had his quirks, but–"

"Stop making excuses for him!" Blain raised his voice. "Why do people do that? Why do we only remember the good after people are gone?"

"It's easier that way," Brooke said in almost a whisper.

"You're better off without him," he said, looking her in the eyes and there was sincerity in his.

"Now you sound like Mollie Sawyer."

Blain's eyes widened. "Well, she would know what it's like to share a life with an SOB."

"What do you mean by that?" Brooke asked, almost feeling amused because she and Tia had a mutual dislike for Freddy, but she never realized outsiders saw through him as well.

"Dr. Sawyer doesn't have too many friends. He's arrogant and anytime I've seen his wife with him, she appears submissive and that burns my ass! A woman, no woman, deserves to be treated that way."

"I completely agree," Brooke said, smiling at him. Blain

Lanning had his faults too, but he was a good man. The timing, however, was ironic when a woman dressed in skin-tight denim, black stilettos, and a dangerously low-cut, paper thin, white sweater walked up to their table.

Her hair was poker straight, stringy, and badly bleached blonde. She looked only at Blain first. "Hey there, Lanning. Didn't think anyone worth a second look would pop in here on the holiday. What do you say we catch up a little later, you know, after your sister leaves?" Blain's face was expressionless. And Brooke's first thought was, *yes, Blain Lanning had his flaws. He defined playboy.*

"Sorry, sweetheart. My friend, not my sister, will be who I'm spending my holiday with." The woman sneered and walked away, obviously miffed or maybe embarrassed.

"You didn't have to chase your girlfriend away on my account," Brooke said, almost feeling sick to her stomach. *Why did she care who Blain Lanning slept with?* Maybe she just felt like he could do better.

"She's not my girlfriend, I don't have a girlfriend," he defended. "I recognized her as the mistress of none other than who we were just talking about."

"Excuse me?" she asked him.

"Doc Sawyer," he clarified.

"You have to be mistaken!" Brooke raised her voice.

"Not many people know, but the little lady likes to talk. Her name is Dee Campbell. One of my buddies told me their affair has been ongoing. The good doctor has been trying to get rid of her, but she has some sort of hold on him."

Brooke still could not process that her best friend, Mollie was being cheated on. She never liked Freddy, but she never thought he would be the type of man, husband, and father, to hurt his family in that way. To cheat. "So she's blackmailing him to sleep with her?"

"I hardly think it started out that way, but I don't know and I don't care," Blain told her.

"Mollie needs to know about this," Brooke sighed, knowing she believed her husband hung the moon. *But, really*, Brook wondered, *was Mollie truly happy with him?* She had changed so much, especially in the last year. She wasn't her bubbly, fun self anymore. Not even when they shared girls' nights with Tia.

"Leave my name out of it. It's only what I've heard secondhand," Blain stated.

"So you've never actually seen them together?" Brooke asked him, pointblank.

"No, but I have seen him waltz in here. His destination, after a drink, was always the BJ room." Brooke looked puzzled, and Blain explained, quietly, "Blowjob," as Brooke felt her face flush and he giggled.

"I had no idea there was such a thing, but I guess I'm out of the loop when it comes to that. It's been a long time," she admitted, as she took the last swallow in her second glass of wine. Blain didn't know what to say to her after that. She was a beautiful, sensual woman, and she was wasting her life away on waiting for a man who, chances were, was not coming back.

"It's time to let go," Blain said, eventually, as he refilled her glass and his again.

"I know that, but I can't convince my heart of it. And, I can't get past not knowing what happened to him. Is he alive? Because if he's not, where the hell is his body? And, if he is out there, does he not want to be found? Who can live with so many unanswered questions?"

"I suppose we just have to learn to accept the fact that we will never know. Live your life. Say goodbye without closure. If you don't, you're wasting a damn good life that I know you could have." Blain's advice stung. She needed to hear those words, but she didn't want to. Not yet. Maybe not ever.

Their shared bottle of Cabernet and both of their glasses were empty, but they continued to sit there, across the table from each other, talking.

"He used to tell me I was the one. He knew it from the moment we met." Brooke had never shared that with anyone before, not even Tia or Mollie. Blain listened raptly as she continued. "I loved him, I still do. I know he and I worked too much and should have taken more time to play and be adventurous, but that wasn't us."

"That wasn't him," Blain interrupted.

"We were happy the way we were," she added.

"Maybe," Blain said, "but he's gone now and it's time for you to live. Live your life how you've always wanted. You only get one, Brooke. Don't waste it mourning a man who is never coming back. I'm also pained by how we will never have answers, but sometimes that's the way life goes." When he stopped talking, he reached across the table for her hand. She felt his soft, gentle grip and something inside of her stirred. And then she panicked. She wasn't ready for this. She didn't want Bryce's younger brother to comfort her and touch her that way. She immediately pulled back and quickly removed her hand from his.

His eyes widened, and then he apologized if he offended her. "I'm sorry, that was not what it seemed. I like you, respect you, Brooke. I'm here for you to lean on, anytime, if you need me. I think you know that by now."

"I do," she responded, making fleeting eye contact between him and her hands which were now on her lap. "We can never be more than that though. Friends, I mean," she told him. "I'm not going to be just another notch on your belt, as they say."

Blain smiled, hoping he was successful at concealing his disappointment. "I think the rumors you've heard, maybe even straight from my big brother's mouth, were untrue."

"So you've never been in the BJ room?" Brooke teased him. If he had, she did not want to know. She was just making an effort to lighten the mood between them. Things had suddenly become awkward, and if she could prevent that from occurring between them, she wanted to.

Blain's face flushed a little and Brooke laughed at him. She thought she had her answer, and she tried not to imagine it. "Give me a little credit, lady," he began. "I always take a woman home first. What I mean is, I sleep in my bed alone. The women I've been with, I've slept in their beds. My bed is pure and waiting for *the one*."

Brooke didn't react to what he said. She wondered if he was telling her the truth. But, she did feel differently about Blain Lanning when he walked her to her vehicle outside, parked adjacent to his, and he wished her a Happy Thanksgiving before watching her drive off.

She only made it two blocks down the road before she realized she did not have her cell phone. She remembered having it out of her handbag, on the table. She thought she had put it in her coat pocket after she bundled up inside the bar, but both of her pockets were empty. She felt a little panicked, hoping it was still sitting on the table, or on the chair, at Ruby's. It was not crowded there, so she assured herself it was fine. She would just drive back and retrieve it.

Blain's powder blue Hummer was gone now and she parked in the same spot she had earlier. She picked up her pace as she walked up to the door again, and stepped inside. The same three men were still sitting at the bar, and this time Dee Campbell was back and flirting with them. Brooke thought again about what Blain had said. *That woman could not be Freddy's mistress. If that were true, Mollie's whole world would explode.*

"Back already?" one of the men spoke outright to her.

"Forgot my phone," she said, glancing quickly over at the table she shared with Blain and she was immediately relieved to spot it sitting on the chair. Their table had not been cleared, as the empty wine bottle and glasses were on it still.

Brooke never said another word to any of them after she grabbed her phone and walked back toward the door. She put her hand on the door handle and pulled it, just as someone else did the same from the outside. The grip on the opposite side was stronger than hers, so Brooke let go. And that's when the door opened, a gust of cold air hit her square in the face, and she was well aware of how wide her eyes were as she was standing toe to toe with Freddy Sawyer.

He looked as taken aback as he felt, but he spoke first. "Brooke! Hi, uh, it's good to see you again." He had not been that chatty or friendly last week when she went to his house to see his wife.

"Happy Thanksgiving, Freddy," Brooke spoke, realizing why he was there. *To see the floozy hanging out of her sweater.*

"You, too," he responded nervously.

"Tell Mollie I'll call her," she added, pushing past him in the open doorway. Freddy never responded, and Brooke never looked back. She and Tia, and even Blain, were right all along. *Mollie had herself a royal son of a bitch.*

CHAPTER 5

It was seven-thirty when Brooke returned to her cabin. The first thing she did after she took off her boots and coat was light a fire in the fireplace. Then, she sat down in the bend of her red sectional and called Mollie.

It took four rings before she answered, sounding out of breath and most likely busy. She still had her hands full with little ones, ages two, four, six, and eight. Her oldest and youngest were boys and she had her girls in the middle. All of her children were blond and beautiful, as they mostly inherited Mollie's features, with the exception of her auburn hair. Any other time, Brooke would not interrupt her on a holiday, but considering she knew Freddy was not at home, she didn't hesitate to call her friend.

After she said hello, Mollie asked Brooke if everything was okay. She knew another holiday had to be difficult for her and she was concerned. "I'm doing well. I spent a few hours with the Lannings, which wasn't easy, but Blain rescued me with Cabernet at Ruby's at the end of the day."

"Blain? You were drinking with him? Alone?" Mollie was instantly alarmed. "Brooke, be careful. Don't get romantically involved with him. He's not the faithful kind."

Brooke immediately thought, *oh dear Lord, neither is your husband.* "No worries, Mol. I'm just calling to see how your Thanksgiving went."

"Good, until Freddy got called into work after dinner. He had an emergency with a patient who isn't recovering well from a recent surgery." Brooke didn't want to hear Freddy's lies. She had seen him at Ruby's, right after dinner. She wanted to tell Mollie instantly, but she knew she couldn't. This was not something that should be revealed over the phone. And Brooke also knew she was going to need back-up support from Tia.

Brooke kept the rest of their conversation light and then she wished Mollie a restful night before ending their call with suggesting how they *must get together again soon.*

Next, Brooke called Tia's number. She knew from talking to her a few days ago that Tia was hosting Thanksgiving for Bo's family. She had invited Brooke to join them, but Brooke declined. She didn't want to try to fit in with a house full of strangers, not even if Bo was one of the best Thanksgiving dinner chef's ever. He prepared everything from baking the turkey to making homemade dressing, green bean casserole, pies, and his added specialty was an odd ball Caesar salad on the side. Brooke had sampled it, the first year she and Bryce spent the holiday together with them, and it was a surprisingly delicious added touch to a Thanksgiving feast.

When Tia answered her phone on the second ring, Brooke could hear in the background that she still had company over. "Did you change your mind and decide you want to crash this wild party?" Tia asked her. "I saved you a bowl of Caesar salad." Brooke smiled into the phone. She sure had good friends. Friends she trusted. Friends who trusted her. And that was why she needed to tell Mollie the truth she discovered about her husband.

"No T, I'm not coming over, but save me the salad for tomorrow," she giggled, before sounding serious again. "I know you have a house full, but I need you to escape upstairs or downstairs for five minutes, I have something urgent to tell you." Tia walked fast through the main floor of her spacious house and went upstairs into her bedroom for privacy. She closed the door tightly behind her and sat down on her bed. The only thought racing through her mind right now was, somehow, someway, Bryce was found. If he was dead, Brooke hadn't sounded upset. If he was miraculously alive, she didn't sound ecstatic either. Tia recognized the emotion in Brooke's voice. She knew her exceptionally well, and she perceived worry.

Brooke was quick to get to the point. "I was at Ruby's tonight with Blain. Long story short, no I'm not sleeping with him, we just had a drink." Tia smiled into the phone. She wished Brooke would let go and have some sort of fun, even if it meant a wild affair with her former lover's brother. "There was a woman in there and Blain knew of her as Freddy's ongoing mistress."

"What? Wait! Mollie's Freddy?" Tia was up and off the end of the bed and frantically pacing in her bedroom. She was the holiday's host in her home today, so she was dolled up in a flattering, fitted, short black dress with three-quarter-length sleeves and a scoop neckline. Her red stilettos were digging into the off-white shag carpet in her bedroom.

"Yes, and at first I just took it as hearsay, or a crazy rumor started by someone who dislikes Freddy, as we do," Brooke explained. "But, then, I saw him come in there with my own eyes. He was caught off guard and nervous. The bar was practically empty, but his whore was there when I walked out as he came in."

"Have you told Mollie?" Tia asked, both concerned and worried about their friend's world which was about to crumble.

"Not yet, I need you with me for that. She's going to lose it and we both need to be her strength." Brooke's hands were trembling as she spoke about it. "I did call her tonight to see how her Thanksgiving was and she explained how Freddy had been paged for an emergency right after dinner. That's exactly the time he walked into Ruby's."

"That son of a bitch," Tia cried out.

"My thoughts exactly," Brooke agreed.

※※※

By Saturday night, Brooke and Tia had a plan in place. It took some persuading for Mollie to agree to another date night.

First, she had mentioned on the phone to Brooke that she and Tia should just go to dinner without her. She explained how Freddy's work schedule had him swamped lately and he sometimes went to his office on the weekends to catch up on paperwork. Brooke rolled her eyes on the opposite end of the phone, and wanted to say, *bastard*. Mollie finally agreed to hire a babysitter for just a few hours once Brooke told her the three of them were going to gather at her cabin for a light dinner and a few drinks. *Nothing fancy, you can wear your sweats*, Brooke had told her, and Mollie was convinced it would be nice to spend some time with them, and much needed for her, again.

Brooke spent most of Saturday cleaning her cabin and she even sorted through a few of her Christmas decorations which she had packed away and had not displayed last year. She still had no interest in decorating a Christmas tree. She just wasn't ready, and she wondered if her Christmas spirit would ever return. Losing Bryce right before the holidays a year ago, pretty much deflated the spirit out of her. She did find a large wreath with a red plaid Christmas ribbon weaved throughout it and a big bow tied at the bottom of it. She knew she would need a ladder if she intended to hang it high on the fireplace. The stone above the hearth reached all the way up to her twelve-foot ceiling. Bringing the ladder inside would mean trekking out in the snow, behind the cabin, to her detached shed. But, after she donned her boots and coat and hiked through at least eight inches of snow, Brooke carefully hung the wreath and was happy she did.

A few minutes before six o'clock, Brooke was wearing dark-washed jeans with flared legs. She still had a lot of weight to regain before her clothes would fit right again, but with a red v-neck sweater and pair of black furry clogs, she was comfortable. Dinner was simmering on the stovetop. She had promised both Tia and Mollie that she would keep the cooking to a minimum, so she only cooked a pot of Clam Chowder, and had four bottles of Cabernet briefly chilling in the refrigerator. Tia had promised to make, or pick up, some dessert. They both knew, however, what this evening was about. It was their time to sit down with Mollie and support her after they revealed to her that her husband was having an affair.

Tia arrived first, and purposely, because she wanted to talk to Brooke alone, before Mollie arrived. Brooke held the door for her as she walked in. She dried the soles of her two-inch, block-heeled over-the-knee black boots on the rug. Brooke grinned at her and shook her head when she took off her coat. She was wearing tight, winter white denim with a matching cashmere turtle neck. Tia smiled back, and then realized she forgot to bring the dessert. "Damn! You remembered it before I did," Tia exclaimed, standing a few feet away from the door. "I swear to you, I had a turtle cheesecake ordered at Flanagan's Bakery downtown!"

"Actually, that didn't occur to me, T. I was just smiling at you because you can't even come to a casual dinner party dressed down. You're starting to look the part of a millionaire." They both giggled and then Brooke invited Tia to sit down on the red sectional in the living room.

"Don't mind if I do!" Tia responded, plopping down in the bend. "It's always so cozy in here. This cabin has such a romantic feel to it," Tia spoke, but caught herself immediately. Her eyes widened, and Brooke smiled and sighed.

"No one's gotten laid here in quite some time," she stated, and was actually able to laugh.

"Maybe it's time you did?" Tia asked, knowing she was treading where Brooke was not ready.

"I think we need to focus on who's getting laid in Mollie's life, not mine. Poor thing, I hate like hell to drop this on her tonight, but she has to know." Brooke successfully changed the subject, and Tia agreed.

"Do you think she knows already? I mean, how could you not know?" Tia was a smart woman, always thinking and analyzing. She believed if her husband was sleeping around, she would know. She also knew, without a doubt, she would castrate him.

But, Mollie was not like Tia. Mollie's focus was on her four children, day in and day out. She had a family to run, and she was blindsided into believing Freddy was wholeheartedly tag-teaming life with her.

"I doubt she knows," Brooke answered. "She would tell us, wouldn't she? She has given up a lot for that man. We know she regrets leaving her nursing career that was barely off the ground when she met Freddy. She loves her kids dearly but, come on, she needs more. They can easily afford to hire a nanny. Freddy just doesn't want Mollie out of the house, and that sickens me."

Tia agreed, "He's going to get what's coming to him."

"Do you think she will leave him?" Brooke asked, wondering what kind of mood Mollie would be in tonight, because in just an hour or so, she was about to feel shattered. It felt strange to Brooke knowing this was the calm before the storm. She herself never had any warning that her life as she knew it would crumble. Bryce was there in the morning, kissed her goodbye she remembered, and never returned that evening. The fact that he was gone without a trace still seemed surreal to her.

"We will convince her to kick his ass to the curb. That is her house, her kids." Tia's strength was admirable, and Brooke wished she had half of it.

When Mollie drove up, Brooke and Tia had already been drinking the first bottle of Cabernet. They both felt as if they needed to get a jumpstart on calming their nerves. Brooke held the door open as Mollie stepped up onto the front porch.

Once inside, Mollie removed her long, black, down coat and slipped out of her light gray, calf-high, sheepskin boots. She was wearing loose-fitted black yoga pants and an oversized pale pink hoodie. "Seriously girls?" she asked, looking at them both dressed in denim and dressy sweaters. Tia especially looked dressed for a night out on the town. "I thought you said I could wear my sweats?"

Mollie looked at Brooke as she shrugged off her concern. "You are fine, you look cozy. Don't pay any attention to Ms. Jackpot over there." They three of them giggled. No matter how successful any of them became, to each other they would always remain Brooke, Tia, and Mollie.

They spent the first forty-five minutes sitting at the kitchen table, eating their soup, sans the dessert afterward, but there was plenty of Cabernet. When they moved to the living room, Mollie sat down on the sectional and chose the bend. The other two sat on each side of her, and all of them were holding their wine glasses. Brooke was the first to start their next subject of conversation.

"How are things at home?" Brooke directed the question to Mollie.

"Hectic, but good," she answered. "If anyone would have told me I'd have four kids by the time I was twenty-eight, I would have laughed at them. I imagined being a nurse for most of my life and maybe getting married and having one or two babies, in my thirties.

"I guess Freddy blew that," Tia chimed in.

"He changed my life, for sure, but in a wonderful way," Mollie defended him.

"Is he watching the kids tonight?" Tia asked her.

"No, I have sitter, because he's working late again," Mollie stated.

"Mol, there's something we need to talk about," Brooke intervened. "It's not something I ever expected to have to tell you, but we're friends for life with no secrets."

"And we support each other through anything," Tia added, as Brooke continued. "On Thanksgiving, I was at Ruby's. I heard something there, and you know how I feel about hearsay. I don't believe it unless I see it. Mollie, I saw Freddy. He met a woman there."

Mollie sat back against the red sectional and rested the base of her wine glass on her thigh as she still held on to it with her hand. "He told me," she replied.

"He confessed to having an affair?" Tia blurted out, and Brooke's eyes widened. *What was she still doing living with that SOB if he had admitted to cheating on her?*

"No, of course not," Mollie smiled, and she seemed unusually calm. "Brooke," she said, looking directly at her sitting to the left of her, "Freddy was concerned that you did get the wrong idea. He was only at the bar to track down the woman you saw because her mother was the patient having complications from surgery. She was readmitted to the hospital alone and when Freddy was on his way home, he stopped at Ruby's because his patient had asked him to. Her daughter was not answering her phone and she knew she was at Ruby's."

"Since when do doctors run all over town hunting down family members?" Tia interjected. "That's lame, Mol! Your husband is lying to you."

Mollie, again remaining exceptionally calm, disagreed. "Freddy and I are good, our marriage is solid. He and I have an active sex life," she added, trying to convince her girlfriends to believe in Freddy as she did. She had fibbed about their sex life, however, just to persuade them that her husband had no reason to cheat. Most nights, she was exhausted from caring for their kids all day long. Or, she just didn't feel sexy and desirable. She carried thirty-five extra pounds of baby weight on her five-five stocky frame the last eight years. Or, Freddy often fell asleep the moment his head hit the pillow after working long hours at the hospital.

Brooke and Tia momentarily looked at each other. There, between them, sat their dearest friend in the world and they believed her husband was lying to her, but she did not. Neither one of them knew where to take this conversation from here.

They didn't want to anger Mollie, but they did wish to beat some sense into her.

"I saw the woman in the bar," Brooke began. "The person I was with goes to Ruby's frequently and he said he sees Freddy in there." Brooke refrained from mentioning the BJ room. "He meets the same woman there. Apparently it's been going on for awhile, at least a year."

"And who is your source, Brooke?" Mollie asked her with a sarcastic tone in her voice. "Blain Lanning? One of Breckenridge's infamous playboys?" It instantly bothered Brooke to hear Blain described that way. It was nothing she had not heard before. She knew it, but when she spent time with him she found that increasingly difficult to believe.

"Yes," Brooke answered. "Look, Mollie, we just need you to open your eyes. Be more aware of where Freddy goes and when. If he says he's working late, check. Go there if you have to."

"You're telling me to spy on my own husband?" Mollie was clearly annoyed now.

"Be nonchalant about it," Tia said, "but you owe it to yourself to find out the truth."

"I already know the truth. My husband told me why he was at Ruby's on Thanksgiving, and I believe him." Mollie tipped back the rest of the Cabernet in her glass, and both Brooke and Tia knew she was finished talking about this.

"Okay," Brooke said. "Just know if anything ever changes, we are both here for you. There will be no judging. We support each other, we always have, and that will never waver."

The conversation was much lighter for the rest of the evening. Brooke nor Tia even mentioned Freddy's name again. Tia purposely waited to leave after Mollie did, because she wanted to talk to Brooke alone again.

"Are you fucking kidding me?" Tia hollered from the red sectional after Brooke closed the door when Mollie stepped off of the front porch of the cabin.

"I know," Brooke immediately responded. "She's crazy for believing him over us, but what else can we do?" Brooke sat down beside Tia and they both had full glasses of Cabernet again.

"We can prove this and nail the bastard," Tia said, adamantly, and the two of them clinked their wine glasses together before each taking a long sip.

✷✷✷

The kids were all asleep when Mollie got home. The babysitter was no longer there as Freddy had sent her home two hours earlier. He was waiting for Mollie upstairs in their bedroom, reclining in a chair in the far corner and watching a late-night talk show on their wall-mounted television.

"You beat me home," Mollie said to him in the dark room as only the television flashed light and she noticed he was wearing his red boxer shorts with a solid navy blue t-shirt, which looked snug over his round belly.

"I did. How was your time with the girls?" Freddy

appeared happy for his wife to have a night out.

"Good to catch up, as always," she responded, walking toward him. She was exhausted and all she wanted to do was strip off her clothes and climb into bed. She knew her two-year-old would be awake early in the morning.

Freddy stared up at the television again, and Mollie spoke. "You need to be more careful." She had Freddy's attention now as he looked away from the television and back at her. "People are talking. They've seen you with your whore."

Freddy laughed aloud before he responded. "Just make sure you always deny it. Make me out to be a wonderful, loving, husband."

"Or what?" Mollie scoffed.

"Or, you will go down with me if anyone were to ever find out the truth." Freddy seemed confident in his threat, as Mollie walked away and into their master bathroom. She closed the door behind her, and put her face in her hands. This wasn't the first time she had to muffle her cries. She was trapped in a marriage with a man who had complete control, and she didn't have the courage to run.

CHAPTER 6

Brooke slept for eight hours after Tia left at midnight. She woke up and walked into the living room and immediately saw what had occurred overnight as she looked out of her open window blinds. The weatherman had predicted a few inches of snow in the early morning hours, and Brooke knew there had been at least eight inches of snow already on the ground last night. When the railing on her front porch was not visible, there was for sure a foot of snow outside of her door. At least it was Sunday, Brooke thought, and she had nowhere she had to be. But, being snowed-in alone had become a lonely feeling for her.

She made her way into the kitchen, in her white fleece robe and fluffy white socks, and started a pot of coffee. After that, she lit the fireplace. There was always plenty of work she could do on her computer, she thought, scrolling through the Facebook newsfeed on her cell phone while sitting at the kitchen table. Brooke noticed she had gotten a friend request. She clicked on it, always feeling excited to maybe reconnect with an old friend or acquaintance. She smiled to herself when she saw his name, and his face inside the small profile picture. Blain Lanning. Cuter than cute. And always a charmer. She accepted his friend request, and then she checked out his timeline.

It wasn't what she had expected. He had a lot of pictures of his black lab, Charlie. His cover photo appeared to be one of him and his friends, both men and women, on a ski trip. There were no pictures of Blain and women with their boobs falling out. There wasn't anything distasteful at all for a man who carried the reputation of a playboy. Brooke clicked out of Facebook, poured her first cup of coffee, held it, and walked back to the bathroom to take a shower.

A few hours later, she was sitting in her office, which was a corner set up in her bedroom, beside her king-sized bed. She had gotten quite a bit of work accomplished and was sipping a third cup of coffee when she heard the noise of a vehicle approaching. Brooke left her bedroom and walked into the living room, and out of the window she noticed the city plow, clearing her lane. She paid a special fee for the City of Breckenridge to include her on the outskirts when they cleared the snow. Any other time, Brooke would have gone back to work, but today she pulled on her snowsuit, boots, coat, and gloves. She found the snow shovel leaning up against the outside of the cabin on the end of the front porch. Her cabin had a large roofed overhang which protected the entire porch, but when the snow was heavy she always had to shovel what blew or drifted. Brooke was busy clearing off the porch, the steps, and the walkway, just as she heard the driver of the snowplow kill the engine near the house after her lane was clear.

Blain Lanning slammed the truck door and walked toward her in his tight, faded denim, tan Carhartt coat and boots, almost up to his knees. No gloves, no hat. Just bare hands and dishwater blond hair, wind-blown all over his head. Brooke hadn't been absolutely sure it was him in the plow truck, but hoped it was.

"Working on a Sunday?" She asked him as he approached the bottom step to her front porch.

"All the days run together when you have winter in Colorado," he smiled.

"I was surprised to see this much had come down overnight," she told him.

"Are you doing okay out here all by yourself? You're all clear now if you need to restock your wine stash," he teased her.

"Coffee, too," she told him. "Can't live without either."

"Try eating a little food," he said. "It will put hair on your chest." He was implying that she needed to be stronger. Her frail frame worried him a little. She never used to look that way. Just in the last year since Bryce disappeared.

"I'm tough enough," she replied, "and besides, you've never seen my chest, so you wouldn't know." She giggled and he raised his eyebrows and grinned as she saw that familiar dimple appear.

A moment later, he stepped up onto her front porch and asked her if she had another shovel.

"No, just one," she replied. "Why don't we both leave the shoveling for later and I'll treat you to a cup of coffee or a glass of wine inside, your choice."

"Too damn early for the strong stuff, I'll take the wine," he teased and they both laughed aloud. Blain closed the door behind him as they stood together on the wide rug in front of the door and began to shed their layers. He was watching her and wondering what it would be like to come home to her every night. His brother used to have it made. But, in Blain's opinion, he never appreciated her enough.

He used the coat rack near the door to hang his coat by the hood, and then followed her into the kitchen, feeling comfort-able as his socks rubbed on the hardwood flooring. It was warm and toasty inside of the cabin and Blain welcomed the break from being in the snow plow for the past six and a half hours.

Brooke poured two cups of coffee. She had taken a clear glass mug out of the cabinet for herself as well, because her other mug was still coffee-filled and sitting on her computer desk in the bedroom.

She sat down at the table with Blain and he spoke first. "The city roads are mainly all clear now if you need anything." He wanted to ask her if she had food in her refrigerator, or how long it's been since she had eaten. But, he didn't want to appear to be too forward.

"I plan to stay put today, I'm actually working," she explained.

"Oh, okay, well that makes two of us then," he smiled at her.

"Have you slept at all?" Brooke asked him, knowing the snow hadn't come down until the wee hours of the morning because she had been awake until a few minutes after midnight.

"A little in the truck," he admitted. "I was at Ruby's when the city called for me to work the roads."

Brooke immediately thought of Freddy and the night she saw him there. She felt sorry for Mollie now, even moreso than before. She believed in her husband and he was a master at covering up his existing deceit with more lies. "The last time I was at Ruby's, with you," she began, "I left my phone behind so I went back, and when I did, Freddy was there to see his mistress."

"How awkward for him," Blain chuckled.

"Oh, he weaseled his way out of it with Mollie. She believes him over me. Tia and I tried to convince her, warn her, but we failed." Brooke looked forlorn. It was obvious to Blain how much she cared about her friends. He admired that about her. He had witnessed how deep her feelings were for his brother, too. Blain knew Brooke loved big. Blain, on the other hand, tried not to. It was easier that way. No one got hurt then.

"He'll get what's coming to him, I'm sure of it," Blain told her. "Just sit back and watch him screw up. Or, next time I see him waltz in Ruby's, I'll snap a picture."

"It makes me sick," Brooke said to him, thinking of the things he does with other women and then goes home to his wife.

"I know, that's because you're a rare kind. A gem." Blain's words touched her heart, but she was hardly pure and she didn't want him painting that picture of her.

"I'm not a nun, if that's what you think," she defended herself. "I dated other men before your brother." Brooke was defensive and Blain grinned at her. "I'm serious!" she added.

"You don't have to convince me," Blain spoke. "I hardly see a nun when I look at you."

"Good," she responded, satisfied.

After he finished his cup of coffee, Blain thanked her and implied that he needed to get back out on the roads when he stood up, went over to the sink to rinse out his coffee cup and then left it in there.

"Are you working all day?" Brooke asked him, almost feeling like she was searching for questions to keep him there a little while longer. She enjoyed his company. She liked not having to be alone. It was more than that, though, and she chose to overlook it.

"No, the roads are pretty much all clear now. You were my last stop, so as long as the snow stays away, I'm done for today." Blain walked over toward the door to slip his coat back on, and then his boots.

"Well, thank you again," Brooke said to him, standing in her living room, wearing her fitted, black yoga pants, and an oversized dark purple hoodie, and her feet were warm and comfortable in thick, purple socks to match. Her long, dark hair was up and tied back in a messy ponytail. She didn't have a drop of makeup on her face except for mascara and eyeliner around her eyes. Blain caught himself thinking, more than once today while being with her, how naturally beautiful she was.

"No thanks necessary, you pay the fee for us to get it done," Blain stated. "I'm just happy to be your snow slave."

She giggled and before he opened the door to leave, she spoke again. "Don't be a stranger."

With his hand on the door knob, he turned back to her. "I'll be at Ruby's later if you care to join me for a drink?"

"I prefer to drink from my stash here," she reminded him.

"I don't drink alone. Never could," he admitted.

"I'm sure there will be ladies more than willing to join you tonight," Brooke said, feeling the jealously pangs inside of her, and again she chose to ignore her feelings.

"And, I'm sure if you walked in, you would have every guy in there trying to buy you a drink and you would just keep brushing 'em off. My brother is to blame for that." Blain was looking directly at her, his eyes bore into hers, when she responded, "On Thanksgiving night, I let a man buy me a bottle of Cabernet." Blain's eyes were lit. He knew what she meant, as he smiled that dimpled smile and walked out of the door of Brooke's cabin.

CHAPTER 7

It was seven o'clock p.m. and Brooke had stayed inside of her cabin the rest of the day and evening. She had accomplished a great deal of work on a Sunday, *but what kind of weekend was that?* The weather kept most people inside on winter days like today, but for Brooke it meant feeling lonely. She was beginning to reach the mindset that she needed to help herself in order to find her way out of this slump. *Yes, she was grieving for a man she lost. No, she did not know if he would ever be found, or return to her by some miracle.* After an entire year of losing herself in grief, loneliness and despair, Brooke was beginning to feel like she did have the strength to move on.

She thought about calling Tia to see if she wanted to meet her in the city for a bite to eat, but then she remembered Mac had a basketball tournament this weekend. Brooke continued to be proud of Tia for loving and raising that boy as her own. Tia and Bo's love story with Mac, as a packaged deal from the beginning, was heartwarming.

Within fifteen minutes, Brooke had touched up her eye makeup and applied a light foundation to her face, and put on some dark lipstick. Her hair was down with loose curls and it reached her shoulders. She dressed in fitted, black denim, a white scoop neck sweater with gray stitching, and a pair of gray boots with thick block heels, reaching just below her knees, to match. She had decided to drive into the city and browse in the markets and stores which were now open late for holiday shoppers. She promised herself she would eat something for dinner while she was out, too. She didn't want to dine in public alone, but there were options to carry-out at almost every restaurant.

Brooke was reminded of how stunning the Victorian style architecture was downtown during the holidays. She always relished in that, but hadn't at all last holiday season when her life was in shambles. She saw people taking carriage rides and with all of the snow and decorations, Brooke had felt as if she stepped into a holiday postcard. This was what Christmas in Breckenridge was all about. The magical feeling of the season swept over Brooke as she walked along on the sidewalk on Main Street. Her office building was not too far, just a few blocks down, but work was the last thing on her mind at the moment. She was grateful she had pushed herself out the door tonight. Hiding away in her cabin on the outskirts of the city easily allowed her to miss out on so much. And, this past year, that was the way she wanted it. She wanted to hide and be a recluse. There was just too much pain to face in her world, and the less she saw and interacted with people, the better she liked it. But, now, Brooke realized she was ready to step back into the land of the living. The festive feeling on the streets tonight had given that back to her.

She purchased a few Christmas crafts to display in her cabin and a wreath for her front door. After she put those items in her SUV, it was nearly nine-thirty. A bite to eat and something warm to drink appealed to her now. All of the shops and restaurants were still open as people were hustling and bustling during the late hours. Brooke sat behind the steering wheel, turned her key in the ignition, and thought about how good she was feeling. Before she shifted her vehicle in reverse, her phone rang. She retrieved it from the cup holder beside her and saw exactly who was calling.

"Hello?" she said, pretending not to have a clue when they both knew she had seen his name to match his number.

"Late-night shopping this time of year is rejuvenating, isn't it?" Blain asked her, and she wondered how he knew. Then, she lifted her eyes up into her rearview mirror and saw the Ruby's neon sign lit on the building which was Breckenridge's most popular bar and grill.

"Spying on me?" she asked him with a smile on her face, sitting alone in her running vehicle with the heat coming from the vents on high speed. Even with gloves on her hands, her fingers still felt cold.

"No, not really," Blain answered. "Just sitting alone by the window at Ruby's, waiting for my dinner and who do I see right across the street, but a beautiful woman shopping like there's no tomorrow. Come see me, or better yet, eat with me." That was an invitation Brooke didn't hesitate to accept. She was hungry and she was in such wonderful spirits. The last thing she wanted to do was go back to her cabin and feel alone and fight falling into that slump of sadness again. She turned off the ignition, stepped her boots down into the snow, and with her phone still held up to her ear, she replied, "Look out the window for my answer."

Blain smiled wide, also with his phone held up to his ear, and from a distance she could see him through the window. Standing in the cold, preparing to walk across the street, she suddenly wasn't affected by the brutal air temperature on a late winter's night in Colorado. The warmth circulating through her body right now was inviting, riveting, and Brooke instantly wanted to hold on to this feeling with everything she had.

The bar was crowded when she walked in, but Blain stood up from his table by the window and he walked over to meet Brooke at the door. "You know how I hate to eat alone," he said to her after he thanked her for joining him.

"I thought that was drink?" she asked, smiling as she removed her gloves and then her coat while she stood by their table.

"That, too," he replied, taking her coat and draping it over the chair beside him. Brooke sat down directly across the tabletop from him. She noticed he was drinking a longneck and then he spoke again. "I hope you're in the mood for Cabernet? I already placed our order. The special tonight is charbroiled cheeseburgers with the works and slaw, and we have two plates coming to us in a few minutes."

Brooke smiled at him. "I never turn away a Cab, and at this point I'm so hungry I could eat the table legs." Blain laughed at her. It was good to know she was getting her appetite back.

"It's crowded in here tonight," she said, looking around as their waitress brought her a glass of Cabernet and she immediately took two sips of it.

"'Tis the season and apparently shoppers have to eat and drink, too," he said. He had been watching her across the street. Something appeared different. She seemed to not just be feeling festive, but alive. The way she carried her body and the expression on her face, and now up close in her eyes, was liberating for Blain to witness. Brooke was making her way back from a tragedy that nearly stole her spirit. Or, at least it had for months on end. A year was a long time to recoil from life.

"Is that what you're out doing tonight as well?" Brooke asked him, knowing better.

"Nope, I have no one to shop for," he replied. "I always pick up something special for my mother, but there's plenty of time for that yet."

"Just your mother? What about all of the women in your life, Blain Lanning?" Brooke asked him, directly. "You can't tell me they don't expect a gift from you under their tree on Christmas morning?"

"There's no one special enough for that craziness, at least not yet," Blain said, taking a long swig of his beer.

"She'll come along eventually," Brooke said, sincerely, and Blain wanted to say, *she already has*, but he refrained as their waitress returned with their two plates of food.

They ate and shared steady conversation until eleven-thirty. There were only a few other tables occupied by the time Brooke suggested they call it a night. "Tomorrow is Monday," she reminded him. Other than being with Tia and Mollie, this was the latest hour Brooke had stayed out in a very long time. She didn't care that tomorrow spearheaded another work week. She had already worked today, on her own free will, and tonight was about getting outside of the box she had trapped herself in for so long.

"I'll take care of the bill," Blain said, as he stood up from his chair and started to walk away from the table.

"No, let it be my treat," Brooke argued, and reached on the chair beside hers to retrieve her wallet inside of her handbag.

"Absolutely not. You bring out the gentleman in me, and I'm kind of enjoying that," he said, walking away from her and she watched him move all the way up to the bar. The tight, faded denim, royal blue flannel shirt, and laced, tan work boots were his trademark. His legs and rear end were muscular. His torso and biceps looked rock hard. And Brooke needed that last drop of Cabernet from her glass. She left it burn in her mouth, on top of her tongue, until her eyes watered a little. *Oh dear Lord, what am I getting myself, deeper and deeper, into?*

Brooke was bundled with her white down coat zipped all the way up underneath her chin, and her gloves were on her hands again. Blain was walking beside her with his bare hands stuffed into his coat pockets. The air was colder than it was two hours earlier and the wind had picked up, too. He walked her to her SUV, swiftly and in sync. He told her he was parked a block down as they reached the driver's side door of her vehicle. "It's freezing out here," she stated, seeing her breath in the dark, but the street lights were shining down on them. "Want me to drive you?"

While he would have liked to have answered, *yes*, because that would give him the opportunity to spend just a little more time with her, even if it was only a few minutes, he declined when he shook his head. "I'm a big boy. You just get in, get warm, and drive home safely." The thought of sending her way out there, to her cabin on the outskirts of the city, pained him this time. He didn't want her to be alone. Not now. Not ever again. He wanted to be the one to share everything with her, life's littlest things and its greatest treasures. But, the last time he had attempted to cross the friendship boundary between them, she was uncomfortable and made her feelings very clear.

Brooke smiled back at him, standing only about two inches taller than her on the snowy city street in Breckenridge. She imagined him stepping closer to her and enveloping her in his strong arms. The seconds were passing by, one after another, and Brooke contemplated asking him to follow her home. *No, not the cabin. Not where she and Bryce shared their lives, and intimacy.* Then, she thought of his loft only four of five blocks away. *But, he never brought women there.* He told her so himself. *Did she really want to be just another woman Blain Lanning laid?* A bitter cold gust of wind nearly took her breath as her thoughts raced and she felt forced to snap out of this mindset and say goodnight.

"Thank you for the late-night dinner, Cabernet, and conversation," she said, gratefully. "I don't know which I loved more."

"Oh, be honest, it's always the Cabernet, hands down," he teased her and stepped toward her. He leaned forward, reached out his arm, and opened her car door for her. She laughed, and then felt a little regretful that she actually momentarily believed Blain was going to take her into his arms and kiss her good night.

He stepped back as he opened the door wide for her to get in, and after she did, she immediately started up the engine and reached to bring the window down before Blain closed her door for her. He bent forward, slightly, and leaned in toward her a little more than she was expecting. His bare hands were now out of his pockets and both were gripping the base of her window.

She started to say, *you're going to freeze*, but he didn't look cold. She wanted to say, *get in, I'll drive you anywhere, just as long as we go there together*. But, she never spoke a word. She didn't have a chance to as Blain slowly moved further inside of her window and toward her lips with his own. She found herself responding. His lips were warm, his tongue tasted like the onions from his burger, and beer too. *Damn, a beer never tasted so good to her.*

Their kiss was over before she knew, and it didn't last as long as she would have loved it to. Blain backed up from the window, and spoke softly, and sounded *sexy*. "Goodnight, Brooke Carey. See you soon, I hope."

He stuffed his hands back into his coat pockets just as she responded, "Tomorrow isn't soon enough."

CHAPTER 8

Brooke never slept all night long, and she was up and out of bed by six o'clock in the morning. She poured her first cup of coffee, walked into the living room and curled up in the corner of her red sectional. She covered her bare legs with the separated ends of her white fleece robe. Blain, and what happened between them, continued to weigh on her mind. Kissing him felt nothing short of amazing, and Brooke wished they would have spent the night together. She wanted to know what it would feel like to be in his arms. Maybe she was just too damn lonely for far too long?

She finished one cup of coffee, and never lit the fireplace because she wanted to get showered, dressed, and out of the door early. She had one stop to make before going to the office.

Next door to *Illusions by TK* on North French Street was Tia's office building for her skincare line. *Reality* had taken off so quickly that she had outgrown her office in the back of the *Illusions by TK* building. The main entrance was open and Brooke walked in to find a secretary and two men in suits, who appeared to be conducting business in the lobby.

Brooke stepped onto the light-colored marble flooring and walked up to the secretary who had already made eye contact with her. "Hi, is Tia in?" Brooke asked, as she noticed the woman behind the desk had what looked like an operator's headset on.

"Do you have an appointment?" she asked, and Brooke told her *no*, just as she looked up to find Tia walking down the long hallway leading into the lobby. As usual, she looked glamorous. An ivory-colored short skirt, over-the-knee boots to match, and a red, cashmere cowl neck sweater. For work today, Brooke had dressed down in skinny jeans, block-heeled black boots which reached her calves, and a white button down long-sleeved blouse which no one could see because she was wearing her white down coat over top.

"Brooke?" Tia spoke first. "Everything okay?" she asked, keeping her voice low while she walked all the way up to her, and stood close.

"Do you have five minutes to talk?" Brooke asked her, and Tia nodded before she told the gentlemen waiting for her that she needed a few more minutes before they could begin their meeting.

Brooke followed Tia back to her spacious office, again with the same marble flooring as in the lobby. All of the furniture was a mix of either black or ivory, and her large desk was glass-topped.

"Sit down with me," Tia offered, leading Brooke to the ivory-colored leather couch along the wall where they sat close.

"I'm sorry, I know you have people waiting for a piece of your time," Brooke began, and Tia noticed something different in her eyes. She seemed less sad. More put together. Maybe even cheerful, or hopeful about something. Or someone.

"They can wait," Tia said. "You never come see me here, so out with it. What's on your mind?" Brooke suddenly felt like a foolish teenager who wanted to tell her best friend she had been kissed by a boy. But, it was more than that. She knew it, and she also believed Tia would see it her way as well. This was about making progress. Letting go. Possibly moving on. Brooke just needed to tell someone, talk it out, and maybe even seek some advice for what to do now.

"You're going to think I've lost my mind, but hear me out first." Tia nodded her head. "I think I'm falling for Blain."

"Bryce's brother?" Tia asked, and this time Brooke nodded. "Then, fall. Feel. Live. Do things you never thought you would ever do." She wanted to add, *just get out of this mourning interlude that seems to have sucked the life out of you*, but she refrained.

Brooke smiled at her. Leave it to Tia to tell her to be daring. "I haven't felt like this in a long time," Brooke began. "It's riveting and frightening at the same time."

"Of course it is," Tia said. "But you can't run away from it." And then she paused before she asked. "So, did you sleep with him yet?"

"No!" Brooke responded. "You know me. I think about things before I *do* them."

Tia smiled at her. "Tell me what's going on then. I thought the two of you hung out as friends, but then again does Breckenridge's playboy know how to be friends with a woman?"

"That's just it," Brooke said. "I've kept myself from feeling anything for him because I don't just want to be someone he has sex with, and I've told him that."

"What was his response?" Tia asked.

"He respects how I feel. But, he did invite me to a late-night dinner last night at Ruby's. I was out shopping on Main and he called me when he saw me from the window. We talked for hours. That's so easy for us to do. Afterward, he walked me to my car, and he kissed me."

Tia wondered if that was just part of Blain's charm, and she felt like cursing him for it, if he was using Brooke. He had to know better. He had to have witnessed how fragile Brooke was in the last year, following Bryce's disappearance. "Do you want my advice?" Tia asked her.

"Hence, why I'm here," Brooke smiled.

"Go for it, but tread lightly," Tia offered.

"I'm not sure what that means," Brooke responded, confused.

"It means don't fall for him. Be with him. Enjoy him. But, keep in the back of your mind that Blain Lanning doesn't commit. He plays."

"I could fall hard for him, T. I can feel it already," she admitted.

"Okay, but don't admit that to him. Only to yourself, and to me," Tia advised her.

"I'm not afraid of a broken heart," Brooke said, while Tia listened raptly for her to continue. "I've had one, and it damn near killed me. Now, I think it's time for me to begin again. I have fun with Blain, and I just want to take this one conversation, one dinner, and one kiss at a time."

"That might be difficult to do," Tia told her. "You can't tell me you haven't already wanted to rip off his clothes? That man is hot."

Brooke giggled. "Oh my goodness, you don't have to point that out to me."

※※※

Brooke spent the entire day at her downtown office, and because she was busy and productive, she didn't have time to think of Blain. She was glad she told Tia, and had been on the receiving end of her helpful feedback. Tia was always her go-to person, moreso than Mollie. Mollie, in recent years, had been too caught up in being a wife and mother. In the past year, since Bryce's disappearance, Brooke had grown closer to Tia and further apart from Mollie. Brooke felt partly to blame for not trying hard enough to stay connected to Mollie, but she also felt as if Mollie was purposely distancing herself from both her and Tia.

On her drive home, Brooke was thinking of both Tia and Mollie. It was the holiday season, and she hoped to get together with them again soon. She recognized the change in herself, and she welcomed it.

Brooke lit the fireplace when she got home to her cabin. She took off her jeans and blouse and dropped them on a pile on the floor beside her bed. She then slipped into her comfortable black yoga pants and an oversized emerald green hoodie. She found some warm socks to match and then went into the kitchen. She opened the refrigerator, but nothing in there appealed to her. She had eaten a good lunch when she picked up a grilled chicken salad at a local pub. Right now, she decided to just pour herself a full glass of Cabernet and sit by the fire.

Just when she got settled on her red sectional with her wine and a blanket, and the television remote control, her cell phone started ringing, and she had left it on the kitchen table. When she reached it, she smiled because, as she had hoped, it was Blain calling.

"Hello there," she said, feeling tingly and giddy to know he had wanted to call her, and he was thinking about her, too.

"Have you had dinner yet, Ms. Carey?" Blain asked, hoping he wasn't too late.

"I actually just poured it," she teased, but it was the truth, and he laughed out loud.

"I mean something substantial, like food," he said on the opposite end of the phone.

"No, but something tells me you have something substantial in mind?" she stated.

"I have take-out sitting on my front seat and I'm about ten minutes away. No more filling up on Cabernet, I'll be there soon." She could almost see him smiling, dimple and all, as they ended their call and she scurried to look in the mirror in the bathroom to check her appearance. She looked comfortable, not sexy, but there wasn't much she could do in less than ten minutes. Her long, dark hair was hanging loose on her shoulders and her makeup which she applied this morning was still intact. She left the bathroom and walked down the hallway, back into the living room. She found her glass of Cabernet on the end table and she took a long swig from it.

When she heard him drive up, she listened for him to step up onto the front porch before she opened the door. He had his hands full, carrying a large paper bag with *Ruby's* printed on the front. "Dinner for two," he said as he stepped inside her warm cabin.

"You're keeping Ruby's in business," she stated. "What's on the menu tonight?" Whatever it was, Brooke thought it smelled delicious when he handed her the bag so he could remove his coat and boots by the door. Then, he followed her into the kitchen where she discovered they were having baked chicken, long grain wild rice, and tossed greens for dinner.

"Eating healthy tonight?" Brooke asked him, delighted with his choice.

"I thought we better watch our figures after those greasy cheeseburgers last night," he said, but believed she needed to gain the weight back she had continued to lose since his brother's disappearance.

Throughout dinner, their conversation was easy again. They talked about their jobs, their food likes and dislikes, and another fierce winter storm that was forecasted to move into Breckenridge in two days.

"This one is predicted to be like last year's crazy one," Blain said, and then he caught himself. That was the night Bryce went missing.

"It's okay," Brooke said, noticing the sudden awkwardness in his facial expression and body language. "We've always been able to talk about him. Why should we stop now?"

"Maybe because I feel a little bit guilty," he answered, honestly.

"Because?" she asked, already knowing why.

"Because I kissed my brother's–"

"I'm not *his* anymore," Brooke interrupted, surprising herself for a moment. "He," for whatever reason, she thought, "is gone."

"And you've reached the point of accepting that?" Blain asked her, realizing she had. There was a definite change in her.

"I think I have, yes," she replied. "I know it's time to anyway." She stood up from the table. She had not eaten everything on her plate, but was finished. She picked up her glass and walked into the living room, and Blain did the same as he followed her.

They sat down, close, in the bend of the red sectional. "Tell me about living here with him," Blain said to her.

"Why?" she asked. "You used to see us together."

"I did," he agreed, "but I never saw him hold you, or touch you, or look at you the way he should have." This was difficult for Blain to bring up, and for Brooke to hear.

"He wasn't always the touchy, feely type," she defended Bryce.

"Oh I know that," Blain said to her. "I also know he could be a jackass. Hard to live with. Hard to love."

"I loved him," Brooke spoke in no uncertain terms.

"But did he love you?" Blain asked her, directly.

"Yes," she stated.

"Did he ever tell you?"

"Sometimes," Brooke admitted. "And, I just knew."

"Don't say his actions made up for his lack of words," Blain told her, and she looked down at the Cabernet in her glass as she held it in her hand. "I know better. I was on the receiving end of his fist a time or two, also."

Brooke's eyes welled up with tears. It had been awhile since she thought of that pain. She had pushed it from her mind, and chose to only remember the good. "It only happened twice," she admitted, still looking down at her glass. Blain wanted to say, *that bastard*, but he forced himself to remain quiet and still, beside her. He could sense that she was finally ready to talk about it.

"He could get angry without much warning," she began. Her voice was quiet. She had spoken of it before, but only to Tia and Mollie. "The first time happened after we had been living together for three months. I don't even know for sure what it stemmed from. He was stressed about work, his car was at the mechanic for maintenance. He needed a ride into town to work. I was getting ready to bring him, but taking too long I guess, and he lost patience. He slammed me against the wall in our bedroom, and I hit my head. I never saw it coming. The anger. The distant look in his eyes. It was over as fast as it happened, and when he saw the fear in my eyes, he apologized profusely. I didn't respond to his words. I left the room, and found myself standing in the kitchen, half-dressed and trembling. I never heard him walk in. I just remember what it felt like to have him hold me, from behind. I've never felt gentleness like that from anyone. I was so confused. Bryce was not a violent man."

"Oh, but he was to those of us who knew him well," Blain spoke. "I hated him for becoming like our father. He promised he wouldn't. We both promised we wouldn't." Brooke looked at Blain, sitting next to her on the sectional. He was staring straight ahead at the fire, flaming high in the fireplace.

"Your father?" she asked him, and he nodded his head.

"Growing up, Bryce and I shared a bedroom, and we could hear him hurting her. She used to tell us to lock our door, and stay in there."

"Oh dear God," Brooke said, covering her mouth with her hand and a few tears sprung from her eyes.

"Once, when I was fifteen, I was big enough to take him. Bryce never made a move to leave our bedroom to help her, but I did. I slammed that son of a bitch to the floor in our living room, and he knew I could have killed him right then and there if I wanted to. He never hit my mother again after that, not when I was there and not that I was ever aware of. I would have known. And, I think she would have told me. The craziest part of all was I don't think she would have minded if I had killed my father that night. She was screaming and crying and worried about me, but not him."

"I'm sitting here, listening to you and I'm thinking I am not that kind of a woman. But, I was," Brooke said. "I stayed. It was months before it happened again, but that time he backhanded me. My lip was bleeding, and I started crying. I told him I was done and he should get the hell out. And, then, I forgave him."

"I'm not sorry he's gone," Blain said, keeping his voice calm and quiet, but he felt incredibly tense and upset.

"I miss the man I loved. I guess a heart can tell a mind a lot of things, especially when you're consumed with grief," Brooke said. "But, I do miss who Bryce was ninety-five percent of the time."

Blain turned sideways on the red sectional and moved closer to her. "You are so much better off without him. Focus on that, and stop looking back."

"I'm beginning to," she admitted. "It's still so hard not knowing what happened to him." Blain was silent. He easily related to her pain. He always had a love-hate relationship with his brother. He missed him at times. But, now, knowing how Bryce hurt this beautiful woman who he had come to care about, sickened him.

Brooke held back her tears that were teetering on her long eyelashes. This had turned into an emotional evening. "I want you to know something," Blain said, reaching for her hand on her lap, and she didn't mind when he held it. "I am not my brother."

She looked at him, and sweetly smiled through her teary eyes. "You can say that again," she said, as he wrapped his strong arms around her and pulled her close. Her head was against his chest, her ear pressing against his soft, powder-blue flannel shirt, and she could hear his heart beating as she tightened her arms around his torso.

They held each other by the fire for most of the evening. They were no longer speaking, but the intensity of their conversation tonight had bonded them. Their connection was undeniably stronger, and their feelings for each other were deepening.

CHAPTER 9

Tia was wiping tears as she stood barefoot on the white shag carpet in the bedroom she shared with her husband of eight years. She remembered Brooke's words to her early this morning when she called her while driving to work. *I didn't want to let go, and I didn't want him to let go of me.*

The pain that Brooke had gone through with Bryce Lanning was still very present. *I'm so glad you are finally opening up about this,* Tia had told Brooke after she had explained how she and Blain connected last night. Tia was grateful to Blain for being there for Brooke. She thought it sounded as if he needed to talk about his brother being abusive as much as Brooke did.

Tia was only wearing her black laced thong and matching bra when Bo opened their bedroom door and walked in. "I forgot my watch," he told her, as he was already dressed in pleated khaki pants and a form fitting black crewneck t-shirt. He was a physical therapist at a private office in Dillon, thirty minutes away. "But, who cares about the time," he smiled, "I got time…" he said, moving toward his wife and kissing her full on the lips while he moved his hands to her partially bare bottom.

"We also have a child waiting downstairs who needs to be brought to school," she reminded him as he cupped her breasts with both of his hands. "Down boy," she teased him and he noticed her eyes were red.

"You okay? You look like you've been crying," Bo backed up and sat down on the end of their bed which had all-white bedding with disheveled sheets and duvet from the night before as Tia had not made it yet.

"I talked to Brooke this morning already and I was just thinking about her pain, and how she may finally be trying to move past it," Tia told him as she stood in front of him, and made no effort to get dressed yet.

"Good," Bo replied. "She has her whole life ahead of her. I'd hate to see her waste years missing a man who was scum." Bo had tried, but he never liked Bryce Lanning. The two of them had zero interests in common, and Bo always thought of Bryce as a pretty boy. He never wanted to go snowmobiling, or even have a beer. And Bo was done with him altogether when Tia told him he had manhandled Brooke. "Don't you wonder if someone offed him?"

"That's the mystery, and as time continues to go by, it looks as if it will remain unsolved," Tia said, believing that.

※※※

Mollie had already driven her two oldest children to school, and returned home with her two youngest. Four-year-old Anna attended half days of pre-kindergarten in the afternoon. She came into the house walking behind her mother while Mollie carried Aiden. When they went into the kitchen, Freddy was dressed and ready for work, looking for breakfast.

"Where's my bacon and eggs?" he asked her, partly teasing.

"I'm sure you could eat after having worked up an appetite last night," she spoke coldly to him, and in vague terms in front of their youngest children. Mollie knew where he was until late last night, in his whore's bed most likely. It sickened her to know she was stuck in her marriage and forced to stand by and watch her husband come and go as he pleased. She truly felt like as if she had no choice. It was too late to reverse the decisions she made that locked her into her marriage.

"Careful, Mol, we have our children present," he scolded her, and she walked out of the kitchen, holding the two-year-old, and followed by the four-year-old. She turned cartoons on the flat screen television mounted on the living room wall and made sure both of her children were content before going back into the kitchen.

Freddy was eating yogurt, straight out of the container with a spoon as he stood against the countertop in his black dress pants, black slip-in dress shoes, and white long-sleeved button-down dress shirt with no tie yet.

Every time he didn't come home until the middle of the night, or the wee hours of the morning, she knew where he had been. "Since you got your fix last night, do you think it will be possible for you to be at home tonight? There's a bad snowstorm predicted, and it's supposed to be worse than the record-breaking one last winter." Regardless of their feelings for each other, Mollie wanted him off the treacherous roads at night. She still had nightmares about him driving in last year's snowstorm.

"I plan to be, but a turn-on is a turn-on and I have needs that you can't meet anymore," he said, callously. "They do have daycare services at the gym, babe. You should sign up the kids so you can work out and get back into the incredible shape you were in when I first met you." Mollie turned her head away, so he would not see the tears welling up in her eyes. Even if she was a size six again, she would never let him touch her.

She regained her composure and then turned back around to face him, and that's when she said, "Never mind. Stay out tonight, get caught in the snowstorm, and maybe if I'm lucky, you'll meet the same fate as Bryce Lanning did."

✲✲✲

It was noontime and the snow was already heavily coming down in Breckenridge. A foot of snow from last week had still not entirely melted, but the roads were clear. In no time, however, the streets and highways would require the plows again.

Blain was sitting in his truck, parked on the outskirts of town. He had already plowed almost four inches from the roads and he included Brooke's lane en route to her cabin again. He wanted her to have no difficulty getting home later. That would be another five hours, for sure, he thought, and knew he would be back to plow again before then.

He shifted his truck into drive, and traveled back into town. He felt solemn today as he thought of the conversation he and Brooke had shared last night. She was a remarkable woman, who didn't deserve what his brother had done. No woman should have to be on the receiving end of that kind of wrath. His mother included. He thought of holding Brooke for hours last night, and suddenly he was looking forward to the crazy snowstorm that had already begun and was predicted not to stop for the next two days. It would give him an excuse to check on Brooke.

❆❆❆

As she made her way, slowly and carefully, on the roads leading to the outskirts of Breckenridge, Brooke smiled to herself, knowing the plow had already been through. She had an uneventful commute, thanks to Blain. As she reached her lane, she took a photograph with her cell phone of its length with her cabin in the background. It looked like a Christmas card. The snow looked beautiful to her. Brooke always said, if she didn't love it, she wouldn't live in Colorado. After she parked near her cabin, she attached that photograph to a text and sent it to Blain with the caption, *If it was you, thank you. I made it safely.*

Before she reached the snow-packed steps, leading up to her front porch, she received a reply from Blain. *Of course it was me. So glad you're home! It's a mess out here.*

Brooke stayed inside, lit a fire, and changed out of her work clothes and into an old pair of faded jeans with holes in the knees and a fitted, long-sleeved white t-shirt. She had warm white socks on her feet and she put them up when she reclined on the end of the red sectional. She set her phone beside her, and then she wondered why. She wasn't waiting on anyone to come home. She had done that for two years. She lived that life, sharing hers with Bryce, and it was good…most of the time.

Now, she had Tia and Mollie, but they had families of their own and were surely waiting on each other to come home and be safe from the storm. Circumstances were forcing Brooke to think too much about Bryce today. As if he was not on her mind enough, she had a client from out of town mention him this morning. He had not known any better, he didn't know her connection to Bryce. He had just seen a flyer posted on a street pole, and thought he would make conversation as they waited for their meeting to begin. *So, what's with the guy posted on the flyers all over town? Missing for a year, huh? Did you know him?*

Brooke momentarily froze. A million and one memories raced through her mind. And then she answered, *I used to.*

The snow falling hard outside of her window made her revert back to the emotions she was feeling that fateful night. She never thought he would not come home, never return. *Where the hell was he? Was it really possible to just vanish as he had? And, what if, he walked back into her life again one day? Would she take him back? Would she resume a life she thought she wanted?*

Maybe she needed to stop living as if Bryce was going to come back to her.

Her phone ringing startled her out of her thoughts. She picked it up and saw it as Tia calling. "Hey T, are you out playing in the snow?"

Tia giggled on the opposite end. "Uh, no, and I hope you aren't either. Did you make it to the cabin okay?"

"Yes, I'm home. Checking up on me?" Brooke asked her.

"Of course, and you know you can come stay with us if you want," Tia offered.

"Oh my gosh, how sweet are you, but I'm staying put," Brooke told her.

"Okay, that's what I thought you would say, but if you change your mind or just want some phone company, you know I'm here." Tia smiled into the phone when Brooke told her she loved her. "And you know I love you," Tia responded and then ended their call.

Brooke thought of Mollie next. She wanted to pick up the phone and talk to her, as she had thought about doing so many times since the night they disagreed about Freddy's character. Mollie would come around, Brooke knew. Even if she believed Freddy over her, Brooke was still her friend for life. Instead of calling, Brooke sent Mollie a text. *Enjoy your kids in all of this snow. Make a snow angel for me. Love you Mol.*

Brooke stared at the fire for what seemed like an hour. She wanted to go into the kitchen for something to eat, or maybe just Cabernet again, but she was too comfortable to move. That is, until she heard the roar of a truck outside, down her lane. A part of her wanted to jump up from her comfortable corner of the red sectional and run to fling open the door and make her way through the blustery wind and snow. But, she refrained from running to him. She waited for the plow to clear her lane, and then she heard the driver kill the engine. That's when she knew for sure it was Blain. Anyone else would have driven off once the job was done.

A few moments later, he knocked. Brooke moved quickly to the door this time, because it was cold and windy outside. When she opened the door, there stood a bundled up Blain. His tan Carhartt coat was zipped, his hood was up, and his hands were shoved into his front pockets.

"You're crazy!" Brooke said, pulling him by the arm and into the cabin as he quickly shut out the cold air and blowing snow.

"I'm working," he smiled, and she told him to shed his coat and boots.

"Well, take a break and I'll get you something to eat or drink," she offered as he moved off the wet rug in his socks.

"Let me guess, you only have coffee or Cabernet?" he teased. "Don't you ever drink water, or tea, or soda for chrissakes?" he was grinning at her and she saw that cute dimple appear again.

"I have whatever you want," she said, waiting for him to answer.

"What I wanted was to check on you, to make sure

you're safe and sound. It's not getting any better out there," he told her.

"Are you working all night?" she asked him.

"Off and on, as needed. I'll probably go home for awhile, but keep the plow truck." Brooke didn't want him to go home, and she decided to speak before she thought too hard or changed her mind.

"Stay here while the storm rides out," she suggested. "I could use the company."

"I've been thinking about him, too. It's another one of those storms, just like that night," Blain said as they walked in unison over to the red sectional and sat down.

"Maybe I should move to a hot and sunny climate?" Brooke said, only teasing him.

"But, you love Colorado," he defended her home for her.

"I know, I'm not going anywhere," she smiled. "I just would like to get past some of the memories. You know, hold tight to the good, and throw out the rest. I want to start living, and loving, and just being. Bryce was the type of man who planned ahead and worked hard and played little. That's not me. It's who I became with him, but it's not really me."

"Get your snowsuit," he told her.

"What?" she asked him.

"Come on, boots, hat, gloves, all of it. Suit up. We are going out to have some fun!"

"You're crazy," she said, getting up off of the couch, and doing it. Just doing it.

"That's the second time you've called me that since I walked in here," he laughed.

"Be right back," she giggled and went in her bedroom to throw on her layers.

✳✳✳

"We only have about an hour of daylight left, so let's do this," Blain said as they walked through the deep snow to the shed behind the cabin. And for the next fifty minutes, she rode on the back of a snowmobile she had never been on before. It was Bryce's. He parked it and not once took it out for a ride. He was always too busy, too tired, or uninterested in doing something out of his routine. Blain used a portable gas tank in the shed to fuel the snowmobile and Brooke could have ridden for hours on the back, with her arms wrapped around him. The snow was beautiful, still coming down and the wind was wild and cold, but the ride through the snow-covered trees was worth it.

When the two of them stepped back into the cabin and onto the rug, they looked at each other and laughed. It was going to require more than just taking off boots and coats to be dry and get warm. Even their eyebrows and eyelashes had snow frozen on them.

"Strip down and get in the shower before you feel the effects of frostbite," he advised her, as she looked at him still standing there, not removing his boots or his layers.

"What? Are you leaving?" she asked him, feeling disappointed but realizing he probably had to return to the roads.

"I should go," he said.

"To work?" she asked, still suited up and feeling wet and cold.

"Home for awhile," he replied. "Listen, you're shivering," he said, taking off her hat, and then unzipping her snowsuit, all the way down. She stared at him, and then caught herself doing so.

"Stay with me," she said, and she heard her own sexy tone. It had been so long since she felt this way.

"I can't, Brooke," he said in what was almost a whisper.

With him still standing close, she took off her gloves, her boots, her snowsuit and she found more wet clothes underneath. She started to unbutton her jeans in front of him, and he instantly turned his head, and simultaneously reached for the door knob.

"Blain Lanning, don't tell me you've ever walked away from an opportunity like this," she tantalized him as he turned and only looked at her. "I'm stripping and practically throwing myself at you, and you want to leave? That doesn't do much for my ego," she said, surprising herself when she confidently removed her jeans and stood in front of him wearing only her fitted, long-sleeved white t-shirt and red thong panties.

"I don't want to leave," he told her, "but I have to."

"Is it Bryce?" she asked him, "because it sure as hell didn't feel like he was on either of our minds the night you kissed me through my car window." Brooke suddenly didn't recognize herself. She was forward and forthright and feeling more like the person she wanted to be.

"It's not him," Blain said. "It's you." Brooke listened raptly. "You are different. You are good. You are not at all like the women I've been with."

"So, now, I'm too good for you?" she asked, feeling somewhat hurt and now humiliated in her underwear, throwing herself at him like she was desperate.

"I want to savor the time we spend together. I want to take baby steps to get to you, and maybe we can make this, whatever this is between us, last for a really long time. I've never felt this way before, Brooke Carey, and I'm scared to lose this feeling. I'm scared if I rip off those sexy red panties and make love to you, things will change between us. I don't want to walk away, and I don't want you to either."

This was the most honest a man had ever been with her. Brooke wanted to cry, because his words were beyond beautiful. This was Breckenridge's playboy. *And he wanted to take things slow with her.*

"You said *make love*," Brooke noted.

"It wouldn't be *sex* with you," he said, looking at her, all of her.

She took three steps toward him, stood up just slightly on her tip toes in her socks, and wrapped her arms around his neck. He was wet and freezing cold. She moved her lips over his, slowly, and he groaned. "You don't listen very well," he whined.

"I just want to feel," she responded. "Make love to me."

CHAPTER 10

"See, isn't this much better than getting naked together?" Blain asked her, as they sat on the white shaggy area rug in front of the fireplace, in their underwear with blankets wrapped around their shoulders. He held up his glass of Cabernet and purposely clinked it with hers.

"Are you even a man?" she said to him, with a twinkle in her eye and a giggle in her voice.

"Uh, hello, don't make me show you," he said, with his dimpled grin.

"I can't seem to!" Brooke replied, laughing.

One hour had passed since the City of Breckenridge was affirmed shut down. Over a foot of snow had fallen since midday and another foot was predicted within the next twenty-four hours. Everyone was advised to stay in their homes, as the city snow plows would not be back on the streets until morning. It was too dangerous to put anyone at risk, and Blain was relieved to have the night off. He had already declared to Brooke that they were snowed-in, and she didn't complain. Since last winter, that had become such a lonely feeling.

They ate what they could find in the cabin, which were eggs to scramble, bread to toast and butter, and Cabernet to drink. Brooke was using the dryer for Blain's clothes, but she had hoped he wouldn't need them tonight.

He was sitting by the fire again in his heather grey boxer briefs, and even with a blanket wrapped around his shoulders and partially covering him, Brooke could see how fit his body was. He didn't have lovies or rolls. Just tight pecks with a six-pack she wanted to put her hands on.

"Stop staring," he said to her as she purposely and slowly took off her blanket and sat closer to him in only her red thong and long-sleeved white t-shirt. She giggled at him, and he asked her if she was getting warm by the fire.

"You could say that," she said, smiling while she moved even closer to him. He sat down his glass, and pulled her onto his lap.

"I want to kiss you," he said, as Brooke's patience ran out. She moved her lips, her tongue, onto his. She made the first move. He responded, slowly, teasing her, and driving her to the brink, and then a passion inside of him erupted, and he gave in.

    He kissed her lips, her face, her neck, her collarbone. He slid his hand up her white-t-shirt and found her breasts. He helped her out of her shirt, and she removed the blanket off of his shoulders. She wanted to feel his bare chest on top of hers, pressed together, melted as one and so close not even air could seep through. His fingers were caressing her nipples, through her white-laced bra. He could feel them harden as he used his other hand to undo the clasp of her bra behind her back. She was free, and he found her with his mouth. He savored touching her, kissing her, all of her. Being with her, not rushing the moment, felt like it was going to end explosively. She reached inside his heather grey boxer-briefs and he sprung up into her hand. He was rock hard and she used her thumb to tease the tip of his manhood. Blain made his way from her breasts to her navel, and then lower. He first felt her with his fingers, sliding them inside of her panties, and then inside of her. One finger, and then the other. She felt ready. More than ready. He moved his fingers out and placed his lips, his tongue there. Brooke was moaning his name, and holding the back of his head, running her fingers through his thick, brownish-blond hair. He wasn't going to stop, he couldn't stop. He liked pleasing her. He held his tongue on her clitoris and she came explosively into his mouth. She immediately pulled him upward and kissed him hard and full on the mouth. She could taste herself and Blain watched her. She slipped off his underwear and then he didn't waste a single second as he plunged inside of her. He filled her, she moaned, he pushed deeper and harder, repeating his thrusts and feeling driven by how aroused she looked and sounded beneath him. She came again, and he did all he could not to lose complete control. He meshed his body against hers. His chest to hers. His lips on hers. His hands were now stroking both of her breasts as he lifted his body upward and gave away. He came inside of her and for the first time in his life, he knew what it felt like to make love to a woman. It wasn't about scoring. There was no rush to get to the thrill of climaxing. This was a woman whose body he wanted to savor. Now and forever.

It was a few minutes afterward before either of them spoke. They lay beside each other, limbs still entangled, and Blain was staring at her. "I think I want to be snowed-in forever," he said, taking her hand in his and moving his fingers around hers before they locked their hands together.

She giggled, and said, "This is Colorado, and that could happen."

"I apologize for losing my willpower," he said, with a crooked grin.

"Oh, baby, I don't think I would have survived the whole night through without doing what we just did," she said, moving her body directly on top of his, and he reached for her, wrapping his arms around her exposed back, and then sliding his hands downward to her bare bottom. "And, I am certain I wanna do it again…"

***

They didn't sleep at all. It was too new, and exciting, and yet peaceful to be together. They stayed in the living room all night long, with blankets on the floor beside the fire. They watched the snow mount through the windows, and they held each other close for hours on end.

When daylight came, they wrapped themselves in blankets and made their way to the kitchen. There wasn't much in the refrigerator so they decided on grilled cheese and coffee for breakfast. Blain made her promise to stock up on groceries when the next winter storm was predicted. Brooke agreed, but only if he would stay with her again.

After they ate, they never made it out of the kitchen without putting their hands all over each other. Their coffee cups, sitting half full on the table, and their plates with only bread crumbs left on them, rattled on the table top as Blain bent her over the table and entered her. Her hands were reaching, grasping on the flat surface for anything as his thrusts became harder and stronger and she cried out his name. He pulled out of her and turned her around. It was too soon for it to be over. She ran the palms of her hands over his tight chest and bent forward to take his nipples, one and then the other, into her mouth. She was gentle and then playfully began biting him. She was driving him wild as she guided him down to the chair and sat on his lap. His entry made her groan and he held her there, moving further inside of her. Again, it was too soon to be over. She moved off of his lap and willingly bent forward onto the table once more while he unhurriedly guided himself inside of her and this time moved slowly in and out. And it was now Blain who cried out Brooke's name this time when, finally, she turned herself around and made her way down onto the chair beside the table as he remained standing. She took him deeply into her mouth and moments later he exploded with a desire which felt as if it would never stop mounting for this woman.

✽✽✽

An hour later, they had showered together and were both dressed. Blain was wearing the same clothes as the night before, standing in the middle of the living room, talking on his cell phone. He had gotten the call. It was time to plow the roads after another ten inches of snow had fallen, and two more were predicted still to come.

"You have to head out, don't you?" Brooke, dressed in jeans and a ribbed white turtle neck as she sat in the bend of her red sectional, regretfully asked him.

"Sure do. The roads are a mess, and people are going to be attempting travel today," he told her. "How about you? Are you working from home?"

"I can," she replied, "or I can get us a thermos of coffee and ride shotgun with you all day?"

Blain smiled wide at her. "That's the best idea you've ever had, well, maybe not as amazing as seducing me by the fire, but you know what I mean." He was teasing her and she leaped into his arms and kissed him full on the lips before she got ready for *their work day*.

CHAPTER 11

Breckenridge was like a ghost town as Blain and Brooke literally plowed their way from the outskirts to downtown. It took them four hours to reach the downtown area, less than ten miles away. It took at least three passes on each street with the eleven-foot wide plow on the truck. Brooke was content sitting beside Blain while he worked to clear the streets in a town with absolutely no activity. There were only two vehicles, one truck and one car, which attempted to make it through the deep snow and ended up getting stuck. Blain rescued both while he instructed Brooke to stay put in the plow truck.

After the second stranded driver was on his way again, Blain returned to Brooke in the truck. She had her hat and gloves on the seat beside her, and her coat unzipped. It was cozy in the truck with the heat on, and she was grateful to be warm each time Blain had to get out of his truck and returned feeling frozen. After the snow had fallen last night, the temperature dropped fifteen degrees and was predicted to remain in the single digits all day.

"People really should just listen and stay home," Blain said, complaining as he got behind the wheel and shifted gears into drive. Brooke was silent for a moment and then she spoke.

"It makes you think of him, doesn't it?" she asked, referring to Bryce. "You wonder if he had car trouble, and needed help that night. You wonder if anyone saw him, and if they did, why didn't they help? If something happened and someone knows something, why haven't they come forward?" Brooke was rambling, and Blain came to a complete stop again and shifted the truck into park.

"I've thought of all of that, and more," he told her. "We know Bryce's truck ran out of gas, but whether that happened with him in it or not, we don't have those answers. "It's just crazy to think someone can be here one minute and gone without a trace the next."

"Thank you," Brooke said to him.

"For what?" he asked her.

"I'm not sure I've ever thanked you for walking through this with me. Really, you've been the one right by my side, grieving too, all along. I'm not sure I've appreciated that, until lately." He removed the glove from his right hand, and he reached for hers. She was warm, and he was cold. She melted the chill on his skin within a matter of seconds. That, ironically, mirrored the effect she had on his heart as well. He was a playboy, not really caring too much about a woman's feelings. Until Brooke.

"You don't have to thank me. Doing anything for you, and with you, is my pleasure." Brooke smiled at him, and leaned over to kiss him. "Now, let's get to work," he said, winking at her, and she sat back against the seat, enjoying the Christmas music on the radio. *I'll be home for Christmas* was playing, and Brooke thought to herself, how she did feel at home with this man. Probably moreso than she had ever felt with his brother.

✲✲✲

By the following day, Breckenridge was operating as normal. Businesses were reopened and it was a work day for most. Brooke was regretful to see Blain leave her cabin, after their two-days of shutting out the world, which was exactly what they had done again after he cleared the streets. They first stopped at his loft downtown for extra clothes, and then retreated out to Brooke's cabin.

Being in Blain's loft would be something Brooke was sure she would never forget. It was a bachelor pad, nonetheless, but it was his and after he showed her around, they ended up in his bed. He made love to her there, and she believed him when he told her she was the first woman he had ever brought home to his bed. She meant that much to him.

Brooke was thinking about Blain as she sat in Hearthstone restaurant downtown Breckenridge. She was still wearing her work clothes, black leggings, a black short skirt with over-the-knee black boots and a burgundy cowl neck sweater, as she had come straight from the office to meet both Tia and Mollie for dinner. It was her idea, and she was happy they both agreed to meet. Whenever something life-changing had occurred in each of their lives, they promised to always share. For Brooke, this step with Blain felt like it was *life-changing* and she couldn't wait any longer to share the news with her girlfriends.

Tia and Mollie arrived at the same time, and from the booth against the wall, Brooke watched the two of them walk in after they had spotted her. Mollie was dressed in flared, charcoal gray corduroy pants, a pale pink v-neck sweater and black clogs. She was carrying her black down coat, while Tia was still bundled in her long, mahogany brown leather coat. She had high-heeled over-the-knee boots to match her coat and she was wearing dark-washed skinny jeans and the same mahogany brown, high-low sweater with a generous scoop neckline.

As Brooke watched them, she couldn't help but see how different they were. Tall and short. Poker straight blonde hair and auburn curls. An obsessively toned body, and an apple-shaped figure. And then there as Brooke. She was in the middle of them in height as she was taller than Mollie at five-five, and at least an inch and a half shorter than Tia at five-eight. Her hair was dark brown, and her figure used to be shapely, but now appeared too thin. Even her breasts had gone down a cup size from a C to a B. Taking better care of herself had gone by the wayside in the last year, but Brooke was determined to change that now. She felt like living again in so many ways, and that was what tonight was about.

Brooke stood and hugged them both, starting with Mollie because Tia was now removing her coat. When they all settled into the booth, with Mollie and Tia on one side and Brooke solo on the opposite, they were studying their mutual friend with the same look of interest. Something was blatantly different about Brooke. The question was, what, or whom, had brought about the change in her. Tia, being more in the loop than Mollie, had the best guess. But, it was Mollie who spoke first.

"Honey, I'm sorry I didn't respond to your text during the snowstorm. We were all home, so I never even thought to have my phone powered on. I hope you didn't feel too isolated," Mollie said, sincerely. Tia caught herself smirking. It was so obvious to her what the glow was all about with Brooke.

"Oh no worries, I was fine, really. I was not alone, and that's why I summoned the two of you here tonight." Brooke glanced at Tia and then back at Mollie. *I've fallen for someone? I'm sleeping with someone? I'm moving on with my life? I'm living in the moment, and just having fun? The sex is like nothing I've ever experienced before?* Brooke wasn't exactly sure how to put it. She hadn't been in the position to say it aloud to anyone yet. "I wasn't alone during the snowstorm," she began. "Blain came out to the cabin to plow my lane, and the weather kept getting worse, the roads were treacherous, the city shut down, and, well, we were snowed-in together."

"Oh my God, that had to be awkward!" Mollie exclaimed as the waitress brought them their first round of Cabernet, which Brooke had previously ordered.

"I don't think awkward is the right descriptive word here, Mol," Tia chimed in, with a giggle.

"Blain and I are getting to know each other, we have been for weeks," Brooke stated. "I wanted him to stay with me, in fact, I asked him to."

"Are you telling us that you're romantically interested in him?" Mollie asked, and Tia remained quiet this time. She enjoyed the change she was seeing in Brooke, and she prayed it would continue. She needed to learn to live, and love, again.

"We passed the point of interested when we took each other's clothes off," Brooke declared, with a crooked grin, and Tia exploded in laughter.

"Holy Christ, Brooke!" Mollie was not pleased. "You are going to get your heart broken. That's what men like Blain do."

Brooke reached across the table, and took Mollie's hand. "Mol, I'm okay, I'm a big girl. I feel better and stronger and more alive than I have in a very long time. You know how hard this last year has been for me. Please, just support me."

Tia put her hand on top of both of theirs. "We do," she said aloud and Mollie looked down at her glass of Cabernet, untouched on the table.

"Blain is very good to me. We understand each other. I promise to be careful," Brooke glanced at Mollie first and then Tia. "I just need to be more, and do more, than just exist. I'm having fun."

"You should!" Tia interjected. "It's time. I, we," Tia looked at Mollie, "are very happy for you!"

"I'm sorry to be such a downer, I know that's not what you need," Mollie spoke. "I just can't hide the fact that I think it's weird because he's Bryce's brother and everyone knows he's screwed half the women at Ruby's."

"Stop it, Mollie!" Tia raised her voice and glared to the side at her.

"No, it's okay. Really, I'm good," Brooke tried to reassure Tia. "I know about his past, but I'm choosing to focus on who he is when we're together. We all have pasts, or secrets, and we all have regrets and things we are just not very proud of. Sometimes those things do not need to be the focus. I'm choosing to look at now and what lies ahead."

"Very well put," Tia told Brooke.

"I will respect that," Mollie said, taking a long sip from her glass. It was the first time she drank tonight, and she wished she could chug it all down at once and instantly feel looped so she would not have to think about what Brooke was getting herself into.

Their dinner of ginger lobster was eaten, and their third round of Cabernet had arrived just as Mollie's cell phone, which she kept close on the tabletop next to her plate, rang. She picked it up, told them it was Freddy, and took the call from him. He was at home, taking care of all of their kids, and the youngest now had a fever. "He's probably teething," Mollie told him, "but I'll be right there." Both Brooke and Tia looked at each other. The man was a doctor. *Could he not handle giving a two-year-old a dose of Ibuprofen and just keep an eye on him for a few hours?*

"I'm sorry girls, but being a mama never ends. I need to go home." Mollie stood up to put on her coat, and both Tia and Brooke stood with her. After she zipped up, and rooted in her handbag for her car keys, they each took turns hugging her warmly. *Drive safe. Hope Aiden feels better soon. Love you.*

As they slid, in unison, back into their separate booths, Tia smiled wide. "I hate it that she got called home, but this gives us a chance to talk alone!"

Brooke grinned, "You don't have to ask. I will tell you. The sex is amazing. He's smokin' hot and I can't get enough of him."

After Tia howled with laughter and caught the attention of a few others dining near them, she spoke. "Well it has been an entire year! Honestly babe, I don't know how you survived without it. It's a part of my regime." They both giggled, sipped some more Cabernet and then Tia's tone turned serious. "So, you're living in the moment, right?" Tia, like Mollie, did have reservations about Blain Lanning.

"I told you at your office, after Blain kissed me for the first time, that I felt as if I could fall for him," Tia nodded her head, and listened. "You basically told me not to fall head over heels and then flat on my face. I believe you told me to *enjoy*, but warned me to *tread lightly* because a man like him doesn't *commit*." Tia was still responding by nodding her head, and this time she took a drink. "He didn't seduce me, if that's what you're thinking. He wanted to leave the cabin during the storm. He claimed I'm different and he likes that, so he didn't want to rush things, in hopes that these feelings will last."

"Are you sure that's not his way of getting women into bed?" Tia asked her.

"I trust him. I trust myself and how I feel right now," Brooke was beaming, and Tia smiled wide at her.

"I love seeing you like this," Tia stated. "It's damn time you're happy."

CHAPTER 12

Brooke walked into Ruby's at nine o'clock. Blain told her he would be there if she wanted to stop by after dinner with her girlfriends. She took him up on his offer, but the crowd at Ruby's was thick and she couldn't immediately spot him.

For a moment, she wished she had texted him so he would have known she was coming. Then, she scanned the crowd again and saw him. From the back, he was bent forward on the corner of the pool table. Tight, faded denim with a gray and red flannel shirt, and those tan, laced work boots. Two teams of two were playing against each other, and Brooke noticed they were all men. She stood back watching him, not knowing the rules of the game, but studying with interest how serious he looked. His teammate slapped him on the back after an apparent good play and Blain turned to find a woman approaching him with a beer in her hand. Brooke watched him take it from her, and she squeezed his bicep on his right arm as Blain winked at her and Brooke read a *thank you* from his lips. Brooke was unnerved, but she knew she shouldn't be. The woman was probably a waitress, but obviously a bar fly in her inexpensive imitation red leather mini skirt and a paper thin black, cotton tank top with her chest spilling out over the top. She watched her touch Blain, a grip which lasted too long with a look that invited him to do more to her than wink at her. Brooke was uncomfortable, but immediately tried to hide it when Blain spotted her. She smiled from afar and watched him hand over his pool stick to a buddy. His teammate looked unhappy, but Blain brushed him off. When he reached her, he spoke first. "Hi, you made it. So good to see you," he said putting an arm around her waist and pulling her closer. He respected her. They were in public, some eyes were watching, and Brooke was different than the others who wanted to be kissed or groped with the intent of flaunting how they were on the receiving end of attention from Blain Lanning.

"Feels good to see you, too," she said, already feeling more at ease about being in his element with him.

"Can I get you a Cab?" he asked her, and she thought of the five glasses she had at dinner.

"I'm borderline loopy from the ones I drank at Hearthside," she admitted with a giggle.

"I can finish my beer," he said holding up the longneck, "and we can get out of here."

"Don't rush," Brooke said, thinking he never asked her how dinner was with her girlfriends, and also how she had no interest in meeting his buddies over by the pool table. The two of them were from different worlds, but alone together they always felt in sync. She caught herself reading too much into the moment, and recalled Tia's words to *just be. Have fun. Live.*

It was too crowded to find a table so they stood talking in the midst of the clusters of people. When Blain's beer bottle was dry, he said he needed to grab his coat over by the bar. Brooke walked with him, and started to zip up her coat and find her gloves in her pocket as Blain now pushed his arms through his own coat. They were smiling and sharing their typical easy conversation when the woman in the red mini skirt found her way up close to Blain, and moved her arms inside of his coat before he had the chance to zip it. Blain's eyes widened, but not nearly as wide as Brooke's, as this intrusive woman kissed the base of Blain's neck and Brooke and everyone else in close proximity heard her ask him if they *were still on for later.*

Blain immediately put his hands on the woman's wrists and guided her back and off of him. "No," he said to her. "There will be no later." She scoffed at him, and replied, "I've heard that line from you before, baby."

Blain let her walk off, and Brooke didn't know what to think. A part of her instantly wanted to be angry because he had not claimed her and announced to the floozy and anyone else listening that she was *his. His what? Girlfriend? Lover? Someone he cared about? Or loved?*

And Blain was worried about what Brooke was thinking, and feeling. He wanted to treat her differently. Respectfully. He didn't want to scare her off with a public display of affection or an announcement that Brooke Carey was with him.

So, all he said was, "Let's go," and they walked out of there together.

This time their vehicles were parked side by side. "Can I follow you home?" he asked her, and she replied, "I'd like that."

✳✳✳

Blain was quiet as he watched her turn on a lamp beside the couch and then move across the room in her skirt and leggings as she bent down to light the fireplace.

"I love this place," he said to her as he walked over to her and stood close in front of the fire, "but we can be together at my loft, too. You know that right?"

"I vividly remember you making me feel quite at home there," she said as she moved her arms around his waistline, and he reached out to hold her in return.

"Can we talk about what happened with Roxy?" he asked, carefully choosing his words, and Brooke felt like saying, *so the hussy has a name*? Instead, she replied, "Yeah, sure."

"I would like to say her actions didn't mean anything to me, but I can't because I need to be honest. It bothered me, and not just because you were there. I don't need that kind of attention, or maybe a better way to put it is, I want your affection. No one else's." Brooke smiled at him, but her memory flashed to watching him wink at Roxy before he knew she had arrived at Ruby's. *It was just a wink. Little old ladies probably receive winks from him as he holds the door for one or two in public.*

"I can give you affection," Brooke said coyly.

"You can?" he asked her, pulling her into a long kiss.

One kiss inevitably led to more and their clothes were again dropping on the floor, by the fire. This time, Brooke stopped him. He looked at her with questions in his eyes and she took him by the hand and led him down the hall. "Are you sure?" he asked her, as they reached the doorway of her bedroom. "I think it's time to give the floor, the couch, and the kitchen table a rest," she said as Blain giggled, and then he pulled her against his bare chest. He was left wearing only his jeans and bare feet as Brooke, down to her matching lacy dark purple panties and bra, led him by the hand, over and onto her bed.

He savored her, every inch of her body, and slowly began to make love to her as if it were their first time all over again. The pillows, sheets, and the duvet beneath them had just been replaced with all new, and the picture in the frame was gone from the nightstand as it had been placed upside down in the drawer below. It was time. She wanted Blain to be a part of her world. And, this, felt like a good way to start.

CHAPTER 13

By the second week in December, much of the same had been happening between Brooke and Blain. They continued to thoroughly enjoy each other, and had gotten to know each other even more. They spent many hours together, enjoying popular restaurants in Breckenridge and its surrounding cities, as well as relishing snowmobile rides, and Blain even taught Brooke how to play pool at Ruby's. They made no effort to hide their relationship, but both of them agreed to wait to tell Blain's parents. Considering Brooke's original place in the Lanning family as Bryce's girlfriend for two years, it was best not to make things awkward. Christmas was only a couple weeks away, and neither Blain nor Brooke wanted to face his mother's disapproval.

In her downtown office, Brooke was thinking about how Blain had phrased his thoughts to her about his mother finding out about them. *I want you in my life, I can't imagine you not being in it, exactly the way you've been for weeks now, but why rush being on the receiving end of condemnation? You know how old school my mother is.* Brooke entirely understood Blain's case in point, because she remembered all too well how dissatisfied Julie Lanning was with her and Bryce for *shacking up together* at her cabin.

Brooke had three computer screens up and running on her desktop, and each screen displayed three different, upcoming, and potentially trendy styles of spring dresses. It was winter in cold Colorado, but her job had always forced her to think ahead and, in this case, think spring. Brooke learned very quickly in the buyer's market how a dress, a pair of shoes, a handbag, had to be selected with the greatest care from among an infinite range of alternatives.

Brooke was a natural at making the ideal purchases of clothing and accessories for retail apparel stores and store chains. She strived at building and maintaining good relationships with suppliers. That was the key part of her job. And her main goal always was to purchase fashions that their target customer base will want to buy. If customers aren't buying the product, the store doesn't turn a profit. Brooke's job forced her to understand the clothing needs, desires, and budget of the store's usual shoppers. This was typically easy for Brooke, but today she was struggling. She was in constant communication with the owner of a boutique in New York City who she and her company supplied. She had started her morning replying to an email from the store owner, and had since been on the phone with him twice. Brooke had always maintained a positive rapport with Lenny Sinkler, but lately he had been a thorn in her side. The very same products were selling at surrounding boutiques and department stores of his caliber. Brooke could not explain it. She suggested his selling price may be too high, and he lost his cool with her. He was a man used to making large sums of money, so reducing prices was not on his radar. His store was smaller than some of the surrounding ones, and Brooke began to wonder if that was becoming his downfall.

She had not received another phone call from Lenny in the last hour, but she was expecting one again. Brooke was scheduled to have an emergency meeting this afternoon with her supervisor and the main boss to discuss Lenny Sinkler and his crisis. She wondered if her superiors would be open to the option of severing their contract as buyers for him, before he fired their company. It would mean money lost, but with the boutiques currently not selling their products well, a profit was not being brought in regardless.

***

When their meeting behind closed doors was adjourned, Brooke was not overjoyed with the outcome. It had been over a year since she traveled for her job. She used to enjoy the frequent need for her to travel as a buyer, but now she wasn't sure. Her bosses had given her a year to grieve and deal with her personal tragedy, and while they still tried to appear sympathetic, Brooke was told in no uncertain terms that she had to go to New York City tomorrow. Brooke was compliant during the meeting and hid the fact that she had lost interest in the travel part of her job. She had become accustomed to being somewhat of a hermit in her cabin.

Now, however, being with Blain appealed to her most, whether they were going out on the town or back at the cabin, alone. Walking to her vehicle to go home, she wondered if that was the reason she didn't want to leave. *Was it because of her new, budding relationship with Blain? How would he feel about her going across the country for business? Would he miss her? Could she trust him?* The last thought raced through her mind, and back again. She tried to push that crazy notion out of her thoughts. *Of course she trusted him. He had not given her a reason not to. But, he was Breckenridge's notorious playboy.* "Was!" she reminded herself, aloud and alone, as she drove home to her cabin.

✳✳✳

"I want you to come see me at the cabin tonight, if you can," Brooke said to Blain when he answered his cell phone after two rings. In the few weeks since they had become *like a couple*, Brooke had not reached out to him. It was always Blain who showed up, called, or sent a text. Brooke avoided this purposely in fear of becoming needy, and she was following Tia's advice. *Go for it, but tread lightly. Just be. Live. Enjoy him, but don't admit to him if you fall for him.*

Brooke had fallen alright, but she had never uttered those three little words to Blain, nor him to her. She was certain if he said it first, she would say it back. *How could she not? It was the truth.* It's how she felt down deep in the core of her heart, and that feeling radiated throughout her entire body each time she was with him, or thinking about him. She was madly in love with Blain Lanning.

"I can," he replied, as he had planned to call her as soon as he got back to his loft after work, and he had just gotten home. "Should I pack an overnight bag?" he grinned into the phone, knowing what her answer would be.

"How is it that you're always jam-packed full of good ideas, Lanning?" Brooke immediately caught herself. She used to call Bryce by his last name, on occasion. She pushed that awkward thought out of her head and told her man to get to her place as soon as he could.

***

When Blain walked inside of her cabin, Brooke was in the back, in her bedroom, with her suitcase laid open on her bed. She was beginning to pack for her three-day trip to New York City. She started to exit her bedroom, but Blain had gotten to the doorway first.

"What are you doing in here?" he asked her, casually, and then he spotted the suitcase on the bed.

"Packing for an official business trip that I was assigned to go on exactly two hours ago," she told him, crinkling her nose.

"Oh," he said, "I guess I forgot how you used to travel. So, you don't want to go?"

"Let's put it this way, I have to go and my superiors believe I'm ready, after a year of feeling like I was in mourning from the turmoil in my life." They were still standing in the doorway of her bedroom and Brooke was watching his face, his eyes, for any reaction from him about her having to go way for a few days.

"Well, I'll miss you," he said, reaching for her waist with both of his hands. "Did you summon me here to take you to the airport tonight?" Now, Brooke could read disappointment on his face.

"No, thank goodness, but I do need a ride there tomorrow morning and a pick up on Sunday afternoon, if you will." She wanted the next three days to fly by. She, more than Blain, was dreading the time apart, or so it appeared.

"You just go and knock 'em dead like you always do," he told her. "I'm proud of you. I'm proud to be with a successful career woman. I'm honored to call you mine." Brooke immediately felt tears spring to her eyes. He had never said anything remotely close to those words to her before. To know he was proud of her was an incredible feeling. But, to hear him define her as being his, made her heart reel as it never had.

"Thank you so much," she said, touching his face with both of her hands and there was scruff from skipping a morning shave. He could see how his words touched her, and he leaned in to kiss her full on the lips. He kissed her long and sweetly and then harder and more aggressively. She backed through the doorway with him guiding her every step of the way to her bed. The suitcase was pushed carelessly onto the floor and the two of them fell back on the maroon duvet. Brooke shared all-white bedding with Bryce. It was pure, and less exciting. The maroon color was the closest she could find to red. It defined how red hot she and Blain could be together. He lost his jeans and flannel shirt in unison with her yoga pants and hoodie hitting the floor. Their underwear soon followed, except for her black lacy bra. He had taken her so hard and sudden that he never paid too much attention to her breasts this time. She didn't mind, and never noticed, because the urge to be joined right then, right there, and fast, was ever present for her, too. Blain was sitting on the back of his legs and Brooke had her legs wrapped tightly around his lower back when he climaxed. She had already done so just moments ago with him thrusting deep inside of her.

"Holy smokes, woman," he sighed as he pulled himself out of her. "You make me feel things I've never felt before." Brooke, at first, giggled, and then she grew serious when she realized he was not referring to the amazing sex they had. "What I mean is," he paused, holding her close as their naked bodies and still trembling limbs were intertwined, "I love you."

"Oh my God, Blain," were the first words to roll off of Brooke's tongue, and then the tears came. "You have no idea how much I love you." He smiled, and kissed her sweetly on the mouth.

"Please don't ever stop," he told her, when they parted lips.

"I won't if you won't," she replied, and he pulled her close again. She already decided she would wait to pack in the morning. She had this man to tend to, beside her, tonight.

CHAPTER 14

After her four-hour plane trip and a taxi ride to her hotel to check in and drop off her luggage, Brooke was in the backseat of another taxi and on her way to meet Lenny Sinkler at his boutique. She was tense about seeing him again, it had been over a year, and this time she felt as if he was done doing business with her. The tone in his voice was just off each time she had spoken with him on the phone, but Brooke knew she had to follow orders from her superiors and try to appease their seller. He had been loyal to their company for sixteen years, eight of which Brooke had worked with him.

The chime above the glass door jingled loudly as Brooke entered. She had her handbag on her arm and her briefcase in her hand. She was wearing fitted black dress pants, black stilettos, and under her long dark pink lined trench coat she was wearing a high low cashmere sweater with a generous scoop neck in the same dark pink color as her coat. Her hair was down to her shoulders in loose curls, her face looked fuller and healthier than it had in months, and she looked beautiful to Lenny when he took her hand and kissed it.

"Always good to see you, Lenny," Brooke said, wishing this man in his early sixties with a lean, fit body, and gray hair gelled and styled all over his head, had not put his lips on her hand. She shrugged off his actions as *this is New York* and smiled at him.

"Come, join me in my office," he said, as she followed him and noticed the store was busy. Busier than she had expected. Maybe he had experienced a lull, and now that Christmas was only a few weeks away, sales would pick up again? She would try to convince him of that, so she could return from this business trip having had success.

Brooke sat down in the black leather chair directly in front of his rectangular desktop. "How was your flight?" he asked her, offering her water, coffee, or something stronger, before he sat down behind his immense desk.

"Long," she replied, requesting a cup of coffee, "but worth the time spent traveling if I can somehow leave you as a happy man after this meeting."

"I'm going under, Brooke," he spoke to her with direct eye contact and held it momentarily before he stood up and helped himself to a scotch from his wet bar along the wall behind his desk. "I have to close before I end up in worse shape than I'm already in."

"But, you specifically blamed me and my choices as your buyer?" Brooke was confused.

"I've met with all of my buyers this week. You're my last. I want to cut our ties without penalty in our contract." Lenny had aged. He not only looked old, but his eyes had lost the spark Brooke never failed to recognize each time she was in his presence.

"I told my superiors you were serious about this. They wanted me to meet with you, face to face, to smooth things over. We had no idea that it's your business, not us." Brooke felt a little used. She had flown across country for what? To hear this business man tell her he's done, and it really had nothing at all to do with her capabilities as a buyer? Brooke was worried about the loss they would take, but at the moment she felt as if she should be more concerned about Lenny. "What happened to you, Lenny? What is really going on? I am sitting here and I'm getting this strange vibe from you. I see the lost look in your eyes, and I recognize that pain. I've been there. You can talk to me. Is this about more than business?"

First, Lenny smiled genuinely at her. "You are the very first client to ask me about me. All the rest have come in here, sat down, and threw up their hands and agreed to walk away. Some were reluctant, but none looked past the business deal and asked about me. You are special, Brooke Carey."

"I'm just a little raw from pain," she told him. "I get that sometimes life knocks us around too harshly and the feeling of wanting to leave it all behind overpowers everything."

Lenny had seen the endless news reports. He knew the story about the Colorado man who disappeared without a trace. And he knew Brooke's connection to him. "Never a single lead?" he asked her.

"Not one," she replied, "but I've finally found a way to pick myself up and move on." She paused. "How did this suddenly become about me? We were talking about you, and what's really going on," Brooke was quick to remind him.

"My wife is gone," he began. "She went missing," he paused and Brooke felt the hair on her forearms stand up, "and was found three days later. She had the beginning stages of dementia and lost her way, trusted a stranger on the street. He's now in custody for her murder."

"Oh dear God, no, Lenny, no," Brooke's eyes were wide as she spoke softly, and placed her coffee on the edge of his desktop and then put her hand over her mouth as she fought to release the tears which had sprung to her eyes. She had no idea. "When did this happen?"

"Eight weeks ago," he answered, and Brooke recalled the woman who stood by his side at so many dinners and special functions. She was a petite woman with cropped salt and pepper hair and a smile that lit up a room. She adored Lenny, and he was mad about her. This pained Brooke, and would have regardless if she had not gone through losing Bryce. Lenny didn't have to worry and wonder for long, only a few days, but the outcome was horrific. Brooke thought of Bryce and that same pain and sadness she had felt for the past year had started to flood back into her heart. She still had no answers. "I know I have to move on," he told Brooke, "but I can't do that here. I need to get away from what we built and loved together. I'm closing and moving, preferably to an isolated island somewhere, anywhere."

"Why won't you try to sell?" Brooke asked him.

"No one wants to run the little boutiques anymore," he spoke with very little drive, and Brooke knew it was time to drop it and allow him to do what he truly felt he needed.

"Well, your little boutique has been very important, and profitable, to me as a buyer in the last eight years. Don't walk away from this believing you have failed. That could not be farther from the truth. You just need to begin again, and find a way to be Lenny Sinkler for the rest of your life, without your beautiful sidekick." Lenny smiled at her, as the memory of his wife still brought him more joy over pain. "I know how that feels, and I also know you need to grasp the things in front of you that make you happy. Hold tight, claw to keep yourself up. Do whatever is necessary to prevent sinking deeper into the quicksand. Believe me, it wants to take you down, but you can't let it."

After two cups of coffee and two hours of conversation, Brooke and Lenny eventually focused on the reason she was there. She signed the agreement contract to null their business dealings. It wasn't the first time she as a buyer had amicably severed ties with a seller, but this time was sad considering she knew Lenny's personal circumstances behind his final decision. She did leave him feeling much better about having to alter his life's plans, and he told her how grateful he was. He invited her to a closing party at his boutique the following evening, and she accepted.

Her heart was heavy when she returned to her hotel. On the drive there, she had watched from the backseat of the taxi how people walked the streets of New York City among oodles of holiday decorations outside of storefronts and businesses. 'Tis the season to put a spring in their steps, but Brooke had felt melancholy when she took off her coat and heels and sat on the end of the king-sized bed in her hotel suite.

Life sure had a cruel way of turning out for some people. *Poor Lenny*, she thought. And, *poor Bryce*. In her heart, she knew he was gone and never coming back. *At least Lenny had closure, but how sad for him.*

Brooke took out her phone and called Blain. If she had gained anything from her conversation with Lenny, it was not to waste a second when you're happy doing something, or being with someone. Brooke thought his phone was going to voicemail when he finally answered. "You're too far away and I miss you already," were the words he used to greet her on the opposite end of the phone, nearly nineteen hundred miles away.

She smiled into the phone. "You better be tucked in your bed in your loft and thinking about me," she teased him.

"It's seven thirty at night, baby, and I'm at my familiar stomping ground," he stated.

"What's the special tonight?" she asked him, feeling hungry as she had not eaten anything since breakfast with Blain at her cabin. They had gotten accustomed to having grilled cheese and coffee after eating it when the kitchen was bare during the snowstorm.

"Greasy cheeseburgers, again," he answered her, and Brooke could hear chatter and music in the background.

"That sounds delicious. I want one again when I get back," she told him as she crisscrossed her legs on the bed and held the phone to her ear.

"Are you still flying home on Sunday, or did you win over your seller already at your meeting today?" Blain liked to talk to her about her career. He never had a desire to go to college or select a career. The city job was available, he needed the money, and he enjoyed the labor.

"No deal on that. Our work together is done, but it's really for the best. No hard feelings at all," Brooke told him.

"Will your bosses be upset?" Blain asked her.

"Not when I explain everything in detail," she responded.

"Tell me more about it when you get back," he said, sounding as if he was hurrying to end their call. She assumed his food had arrived or someone was there he knew.

"I will. I'll let you go, and I'll call you again tomorrow." Brooke planned to take advantage of being in New York City and pay unexpected visits to several of their other stores where they had retail on the racks.

"Okay, be safe and enjoy your stay there. I've never been to NYC," he said.

"Go with me sometime," she offered. "It'll be fun."

"Anywhere with you is fun," he replied and then he heard her say, *Awe*.

***

The following day turned out to be exceptionally busy, and as fast-paced as New York City was known to be. The crazy traffic and people walking everywhere to get there faster, even in the cold temperatures, made Brooke miss her laid-back life in the Colorado cabin. She enjoyed herself at the closing party at Lenny's boutique, where she had worn a long, sleek sleeveless black dress with a plunging neckline, and red stilettos. She did leave early at a few minutes after eleven, but not before she had pulled Lenny aside when the party was still in full swing, and told him goodbye.

Brooke slipped out of her heels and her long dress and right into the hotel bed, still wearing her matching red lacy bra and thong. She reached for her phone on the nightstand and sent Blain a text. It was nearly midnight in New York City and only going on ten o'clock in Colorado. She knew Blain was playing pool tonight, and she didn't want to interrupt the game with a phone call. Brooke sent a quick, but sweet text to him. *Can't hardly wait to get on that plane in the morning and have it bring me back to you. Good night. I love you.*

Brooke tossed in the strange bed for almost an hour. Finally, she opened her eyes, reached for her phone again and decided to open up Facebook. She scrolled the newsfeed for about ten minutes. Tia and Bo had taken a date night selfie and more than one hundred people had liked it and half as many had commented on what a *beautiful couple* they were. Brooke *liked* it too, and then scrolled below it and was surprised to see Blain was tagged in a post. She knew he was rarely on Facebook, because they had talked about it after he had sent her a friend request, before they became lovers. There was no picture, just a post which read *Thank you for a wonderful night last night, Blain Lanning. You sure know how to lift a girl up when she's down.* A red heart followed that message, and Brooke swallowed hard. The name of the woman who posted, and tagged Blain, was Dee Campbell. She was Freddy Sawyer's whore. *What in the hell was Blain doing with her? God, no…*

CHAPTER 15

Brooke never slept at all, and she was distraught in her thoughts for the entire four-hour plane ride. She had not heard from Blain. He never responded to her text last night. She kept checking Facebook to see if Blain would like or comment on the post he was tagged in, but there was nothing new. Just the same three likes and zero comments.

She was going to confront him about the post. She had to. She had to know what Dee Campbell meant and why he was with her. She wanted to trust him, but the more she dwelled on what she read, the less she did.

This was what Mollie and Tia had forewarned her about. *Blain was a playboy. Don't let him into your world. If you do, just have fun, don't fall for him.* Their mix of advice was circling around in her mind as Brooke stepped off the plane. He was supposed to meet her there, at the airport at four-thirty and her plane was on time.

She spotted him in the crowd after she had retrieved her one suitcase. He hurried toward her and picked her up swiftly into his arms, suitcase and all. She embraced him back, tightly. She closed her eyes tightly, too. She didn't want to believe it. Not Blain. Not the man who had shown her how to move on, and love again.

"You look amazing!" he said, setting her back down on her feet and taking a long look at her with a wide smile on his face.

"Thank you," she responded.

"I'm so glad you're on time," he said, looking relieved. "I lost my phone last night, and I was worried you had tried to call or text and I didn't get it."

"I did text you last night, just to say goodnight," she said to him as they were still standing in the middle of the airport and the people continued to hustle by them. "How did you lose your phone?"

"I don't know exactly," he attempted to explain, and she frowned at him. *Had he left it at Dee Campbell's place? Or, in that pornographic backroom of the bar?* "I helped out a stranger, stranded alongside of the road last night, and I think I lost it out there. I went back today but I can't find it in the snow. We got at least three more inches overnight."

Brooke was watching him. He seemed casual and calm. Could he really be lying to her?

"Stranger?" she asked. "You've never met a stranger in Breckenridge."

He laughed, "Well, she's not my friend so I wasn't sure what to call her."

"She?" Brooke questioned him.

"Freddy's mistress," he responded.

"Dee Campbell," Brooke spoke. "What exactly did you do for her?"

"Brooke, you sound as if you're accusing me of something," Blain suddenly appeared hurt, and a little miffed.

"I saw her post on Facebook," she told him.

"What post?" he demanded to know.

"She tagged you, and thanked you for the wonderful night. Apparently you lifted you her up when she was down."

"Oh, Jesus! Is anything sacred? Why do some people insist on posting each time they take a shit?" Blain was angry, and embarrassed, and suddenly terribly worried about the conclusion Brooke was obviously coming to with this. Brooke only stared at him, and he spoke again. "Let's talk about this at home." He made it sound as if they lived together, and shared all of the things she had already allowed herself to dream about having and doing with him.

They walked through the airport in silence. Blain had taken her suitcase from her and carried it for her. When they reached his Hummer, he started it up, set the heat on high and turned to her. "I was driving my plow, working to clear the streets of the snow that had fallen last night. I cut my pool game short to go to work. I came across a car on the side of the road with Dee Campbell out of it, flagging me down. She had stalled. I tried jumper cables, but her damn car was just done. Too old, I guess. So, she called a tow truck and I drove her home."

"That's all?" Brooke asked. "Did you walk her inside?"

"No," Blain replied without hesitation.

"Did she come on to you in any way, shape, or form?" Brooke was adamant about knowing every single detail.

"Of course she did," he replied, "but I ignored her. She and Freddy seem to be on the outs so, yes, she was looking for some action, but she didn't get a second look from me!" Brooke was silent. She wanted to believe him, and she did.

"I'm sorry," Brooke began, "for doubting you."

"I need you to trust me," he said, with obvious hurt in his eyes.

"I do, and I had up until when I logged onto Facebook last night," she admitted. "Blaine, you are a ladies' man," she said, phrasing her words carefully.

"I used to be a man who was just looking to have fun with no commitment," he said, "and then I fell in love with a woman who gives me a reason, day after day, to only want her.

I love you, Brooke Carey, and I only want you. Please get that through your beautiful head."

"I'll need some convincing," she said, with tears spilling over in her eyes.

"I can do that," he said, shifting his Hummer into reverse to take her home.

***

The seed had been planted, but Brooke chose to bury it and not look back or nurture it with doubt to help it grow. A week had gone by and Brooke and Blain were living as they had before her trip to New York City.

After work on Friday, Brooke agreed to meet Blain at Ruby's for dinner. He promised her that greasy cheeseburger she was craving. When Brooke arrived first, she ordered for them at the bar, and then requested a glass of Cabernet which she took with her to an empty table in the corner. The place was busy, but not yet as packed as it could get at night. Brooke had just taken off her coat and sat down when a woman walked up to her table. She tried to hide the disgust on her face when she recognized her as Dee Campbell. She didn't this like woman for who she was to Freddy, and what their involvement would eventually do to Mollie once she believed the hurtful truth. She also didn't like her for the distance she temporarily brought between her and Blain. She had come onto him, Brooke knew that for a fact, and a part of her wanted to stand up from her chair and stand up to this woman.

"Hello, Brooke," Dee Campbell spoke first, and Brooke was unnerved that she knew her name.

"Is there something you wanted?" Brooke asked, fully realizing how snooty she sounded.

"Yeah, to tell you that I found Blain's cell phone at my place. It ended up under my bed, and I first found it last night. I had no idea it was there, so if you could please return it to–"

"You're lying!" Brooke interrupted her and had raised her voice enough to catch the attention of a few others close by.

"I think Blain is the one who's lying, honey," Dee Campbell spoke, confidently, and followed by setting the phone down on the table and attempting to walk away.

Brooke immediately stood up and blocked her path. "He's mine," Brooke told her in no uncertain terms, and Dee Campbell scoffed at her.

"I think any person with eyes in Breckenridge can see that Blain Lanning doesn't belong to anyone. He likes to be shared." Brooke's face flushed and she could feel her hands trembling. She was mad as hell, and if this woman was telling the truth she was about to hurt like hell.

"You're pathetic!" Brooke told her, trying to hold it together.

"Oh, no," Dee Campbell replied. "You're the one everyone feels sorry for. First, you lost Bryce Lanning, and I do mean *lost*, and now you're clinging to his brother. If you can no longer take your panties off for one brother, may as well do it for the other."

Brooke shoved Dee away from her with both of her hands. She had never done anything like that before. She felt pushed to her limits. Dee Campbell quickly recovered her balance and bolted toward Brooke. And that's when she was grabbed from behind by Blain. "What the hell is going on here?" he spoke to them both, and then let go of Dee Campbell.

"Your girlfriend is touchy tonight. It seems she doesn't like when I bring up the fact that she's screwed both of the Lanning boys." Dee Campbell smirked, and Blain kept his voice low, but made sure she got the message. "You're trouble. Take note of something. The next time I see you alongside of the road, be prepared to freeze to death."

After Dee stormed off, Blain attempted to comfort Brooke. "No," she said. "Not here. Here's your phone. I'm going home." Brooke never took the time to put on her coat. She just grabbed it off of the chair, along with her handbag, and hurried out of there. Blain immediately followed her.

Brooke started crying on the drive home. She could see him in her rearview mirror, driving directly behind her. *This had to stop. This doubt. These questions. She either trusted him or she didn't.*

She walked into her cabin and Blain followed on her heels. Their ritual of taking off their boots, coats, gloves and then starting a fire was no different tonight. But, both of them hated the presence of silence between them in the chilly cabin.

"She found your phone," Brooke spoke, breaking the quiet.

"Don't need it, I already bought a new one," he told her.

"She said she found it underneath her bed." Brooke nearly choked on the words.

"That's bullshit!" he raised his voice. "Stop believing what you already know could not be true."

"But, that's just it, I don't know," Brooke said, sadly. "I knew you, first, as Bryce's younger brother, and you were the wild one. A man, who your brother told me, had a different woman in his bed every night."

"Stop right there," Blain spoke adamantly. "You know the truth about *my* bed and who's been in it."

"You know what I mean," Brooke said, trying to focus on how special she felt when he took her home to his loft and they made love in his bed. "It's true, isn't it? You've been with a lot of women, in *their* beds, or in the back rooms of the bars. You're a playboy and men like you don't change."

"Is that how you really feel about me?" Blain asked her, feeling deeply crushed by her words. He respected her, and he thought she respected him as well.

"I don't know how to feel anymore," she admitted, with tears rolling off of her cheeks.

"I was not in Dee Campbell's, or anyone else's bed, while you were away. I have not been with another woman since we gave ourselves to each other. If you do not believe me, there is nothing more to say. If you do not trust me, then there's no reason for me to be here."

Brooke's tears fell harder. She tried to say she needed time. Then, she wanted to say she did trust him, and would from here on. But, the words never came. It was as if she was watching herself, out of her body, as she turned toward the fire with her arms folded across her chest, and her back to Blain. She hit her knees on the floor as she fell to them and sobbed when he walked out of the door to her cabin. She had never heard it slam like that before.

CHAPTER 16

Brooke curled up on the red sectional and drank one glass of wine after another. She cried from the ache of her heartbreak, and for the questions she still had. *Was she wrong to waver in trusting Blain?* She loved him, she was certain of that. But, she had loved Bryce, too, and he caused her pain as well.

She was trying not to return to that slump again, but kept drinking and crying for almost two hours. It was getting dark and Brooke was feeling overtired. She had not slept at all the night before in New York, and now she was spent from traveling, and stressed from having the falling out with Blain. *Was it over?* That was her last thought as she laid her empty glass sideways on her stomach and closed her teary eyes. Not more than a half an hour passed, and Brooke woke up to the noise of what she thought were two car doors slamming. She sat up straight on the couch just as her glass rolled off of her stomach and hit the hardwood floor and shattered. Before she cursed or attempted to move around the broken pieces of glass, she heard a loud knock on her door.

"Brooke, open up, it's Blain!"

Brooke made her way around the glass on the floor, and over to the door. She had entirely too much to drink, and she had sat upright too quickly. Her head felt light and it was difficult to focus on the door handle in order to place her hand on it and turn it. But, when she did, she was staring directly at Blain with Dee Campbell.

"What is she doing here?" were the first words out of Brooke's mouth as she stood there in her now cold bare feet, dark-washed skinny jeans, and a white chunky turtleneck sweater. She had not changed her clothes since she came from the airport. Her hair, hanging down to her shoulders today, was disheveled on her head and her mascara had run from her eyes along with her tears and dried on her face.

Blain pushed his way inside of the cabin and looked back with a glare to make sure Dee Campbell followed him. The three of them never moved from the doorway once Blain reached back to shut the door when Dee Campbell stepped inside the cabin after lagging behind him.

"She has something to say," Blain said, giving her a stern cue to speak.

"I didn't find the phone at my place," she said, rolling her eyes, and standing there in a short black leather skirt, black boots, and a low-cut lime green sweater underneath a black leather coat. She looked sleazy to Brooke, and obviously cold with her bare, white legs visible. "He dropped it out of his coat pocket, in the snow, when he was trying to start my car alongside the road."

"And why did you pick it up and keep it?" Blain interjected, firmly.

"Because I'm a bitch, apparently. Isn't that what you just screamed at me while we were driving here?" Dee Campbell was a piece of work, and Brooke's eyes were wide looking at her, and then at Blain. "I hid the phone, intending to use it to make you think Blain was sleeping around."

"Why would you do that?" Brooke raised her voice, feeling infuriated, but she also suddenly felt so incredibly good knowing the story of Blain being in another woman's bedroom was a lie.

"Why not? You're too good for him. He doesn't belong here." Dee Campbell started to say more, but Blain raised his voice.

"That is enough! We don't care what you think!" Blain's eyes were cold, and Brooke knew he had had enough of her craziness.

"Oh, I would rethink that last comment if I were you, both of you," Dee Campbell stated. "You never know how helpful a person like me could be."

"What does that even mean?" Brooke asked her. "I think you've done enough damage, and you're also the last person on earth I would ever turn to for help. You're just damn lucky Blain has a good heart and stopped to help you, stranded on the side of the road in the snow and the cold."

"I agree. Sometimes no one comes along, and people are unfortunately left to fend for themselves and struggle for survival. Some never make it out alive. Some, disappear entirely and without a trace. Or do they? Someone always sees something, no matter where you are or what you're doing..." She had started to ramble, but both Blaine and Brooke knew who she was referring to. She was an evil person, only out to hurt them some more, and they weren't falling for her games this time.

Blain pulled out his new cell phone from his coat pocket and put it to his ear. Both women heard him call for a taxi. When he hung up, he told Dee Campbell to, *get the hell out.*

"It's freezing out there, and I have no pants on!" she balked at him, but looked afraid of him.

"I don't care. You should think before you get dressed. It's winter in Colorado for chrissakes!" Blain abruptly opened the door and the cold air blew in. Brooke again wished she had been wearing socks.

When Dee Campbell stepped onto the cabin's snowy front porch, Blain slammed the door shut. "Are you seriously going to leave her to wait out there?" Brooke asked him, and he responded, "The taxi driver told me he will be here in less than five minutes. She will be fine."

After the two of them heard the taxi drive off with Dee Campbell in the backseat, Brooke left Blaine's side at the doorway and went into the kitchen to get the trash basket. She came back to find him, kneeling on the floor and carefully picking up the larger pieces of glass.

"Did you slam your glass against the wall after I left?" he

asked her, placing the glass pieces inside of the trash basket she was holding.

"No, it wasn't like that," she replied. "I needed that glass to drown my sorrows. It was empty and on top of me when I fell asleep. I was startled when you came back and that's when the glass rolled and broke."

"So, it was my fault," he said, smiling at her.

"I'm glad you came back," she told him, feeling as if she had been on an emotional roller coaster the past twenty-four hours.

"There was no way I was going to let her get by with lying," he stated.

"And what about me? I didn't trust you," she said, wondering if they could get past this hurtful snag in their relationship.

"I don't know," he began, and she tried not to look disappointed. "I don't know what more it's going to take for you to believe I am not the man I used to be. I know I'm not my brother, I'm just not the man he was. He's probably only been with one other woman besides you." Brooke knew that was the truth, and she stopped Blain from speaking further.

"You're right," she told him. "You are not Bryce, and you never will be. You are kind and gentle and hard and sexy, and I wouldn't have you any other way. I mean that."

"Did you say hard?" he teased her, as they stood near the broken glass still on hardwood floor at their feet.

"Rock hard," she replied, grinning. *This was what she loved about him, about them. They were fun together.*

"My body?" he asked.

"Oh yeah, and its parts," she giggled.

"I'm yours, if you want me," he told her, becoming serious again. "I swear being with you, and only you, is something I want with my entire being."

Brooke believed him. And she reached both of her hands out and held his. "We are two very different people, but our souls are one in the same. I feel it, and I know you do, too. I can't, and I won't, let you go."

Blain pulled her close and they held each other with overwhelming feelings of gratitude, which neither one of them had ever experienced before. They had gone through the fear of losing love tonight, but found their way back into each other's arms. And that's where they both intended to stay.

✳✳✳

Two days later, Brooke was at her office downtown. She was on her desk phone with a seller when she heard her cell phone ringing. She reached for it as she continued to speak into her desk phone. Tia was calling her. Brooke silenced the call, and made a mental note to call her back when the pace of her work day slowed.

As Brooke continued to talk, her phone screen lit up. Now, she had received a text from Tia. It read, *call me*, and Brooke continued with the business at hand.

It was an hour and a half later before Brooke had the chance to call Tia. She sat behind her desk, and did so while she bit into an apple she had brought along with her today. Her stomach growled loudly, as she had not yet taken the time to eat, and then she heard Tia answer after the second ring.

"I know you're busy, I am too, but we need to talk," Tia spoke fast into the phone and Brooke wondered if she should be worried. Brooke replied, "Okay, what's going on?" as Tia continued. "Bo was at Ruby's last night for some kind of happy hour, going away dinner celebration, for a therapist at his office. He came home and said things got a little heated there between Freddy and his mistress."

"Oh dear God, in public?" Brooke blurted out.

"No, not that kind of heat," Tia corrected her. "They fought."

"I did hear they were on the outs," Brooke said, remembering Blain telling her so when he told her the story of helping her alongside of the road. She felt repulsed thinking about the irreversible damage Dee Campbell's lie almost did to her and Blain.

"Well, she had entirely too much to drink. Bo was watching them together, and he doesn't think Freddy knew he was there. They started to argue and she ended up throwing her drink at him, splashing him in the face, and his only reaction was to walk away, but she wouldn't let him. She wanted his attention so badly that she raised her voice and yelled out something that pretty much caught the attention of the whole place. She said, 'I own you and I have a dead man to thank for that.'"

"Holy crap!" Brooke responded. "What happened after that?"

"Bo said that Freddy grabbed her and dragged her into one of the back rooms of the bar."

"That must have been some scene," Brooke said, believing Tia was telling her this in urgency because of Mollie. She was certain Mollie either already knew, or would hear about it. Exactly what it meant, or how true Dee Campbell's words were, was not something Brooke was focused on or cared about.

"It was, and afterward Bo said it's all everyone at his table kept talking about. It didn't occur to Bo, but he said one of his co-workers brought up Bryce."

"What about Bryce?" Brooke asked, honesty confused.

"Do you think Freddy knows something about what happened to him that night?" Tia asked, still feeling shaken about Bo's insistence that this should be brought to the attention of the police detectives on Bryce's case.

"Oh that's absurd," Brooke said, without question. "Besides, Dee Campbell is a lying bitch." Brooke proceeded to update Tia on what had happened when she was in New York City on business. Tia could hear the disgust in Brooke's voice. She also picked up on just how serious Brooke had quickly become about Blain Lanning.

"You're in pretty deep with him, if you're declaring love already," Tia said, worried about Brooke. She wondered if a man like Blain could remain faithful.

"As deep as it gets," Brooke responded.

"Just be careful," Tia told her, pushing aside the initial reason she had called her today, and Brooke responded, "I've got this."

CHAPTER 17

Brooke couldn't stop thinking about what Tia told her on the phone. For an entire year, she had worried, wondered, and contemplated what could have happened to Bryce that night. But, for awhile now, she had finally been able to put it out of her mind. She no longer thought about him, day in and day out. The pain was still there, but the loneliness and the tears were finally gone. She had found a way to move forward, and she credited Blain. They helped each other to heal, and they had accepted together that they just might not ever know what happened.

Blain walked into the cabin and found Brooke staring at the fire from the bend of the red sectional. It was obvious to him that she had been lost in her thoughts.

"Hi," she said to him as she sat there still in her gold skirt, black leggings, and oversized ivory tunic, which she had worn to work.

"What are you thinking about over there?" Blain asked as he removed his boots by the door, and then walked over to her in socks.

"Bryce," she answered, and Blain's eyes widened.

"That's okay," Blain said, sitting down beside her. "It happens to me, too."

"It's not what you think," she told him. "I mean, I miss him for many reasons, but I'm moving on."

"It's nice to be able to do that, isn't it?" Blain asked her. "It's simply nice not to dwell so much on what happened, or what could have been."

"I love you, Blain," she said, reaching for his hand.

"I know that," he said, intertwining his fingers with hers. "And, I love you. That doesn't mean you can't still grieve and miss Bryce, okay?"

"Okay," she said, smiling at him. They were silent for a few minutes, watching the fire together, and then Brooke spoke again. "I heard something today. It seems that Dee Campbell caused quite a ruckus at Ruby's. She has the town whispering, and Bryce's name came up." Blain listened as she continued.

"She was drunk and arguing loudly with Freddy. He started to leave and she yelled out something about owning him and having a dead man to thank for it."

"What? Is this a rumor?" Blain asked, not really wanting to spend their time together discussing Dee Campbell.

"Tia's husband, Bo was there. He said people were intrigued, and thought maybe the police should be called. The missing person flyers are still all over town. It's been a year, but the mystery of Bryce's disappearance still lingers."

"Do you believe this?" Blain asked. "Do you really think the Coward of the County, Freddy Sawyer, knows something about Bryce?"

"No, but why would Dee Campbell say she owned him and then mention a dead person?" Tia asked.

"First, why does Dee Campbell say and do half the things she does?" Blain asked. "And, second, you and I both know she has no credibility."

"You're right. I shouldn't even give her a second thought," Brooke said.

"That's the best idea you've had since I got here," he teased her, and she laughed. And, just like that, the subject was dropped.

❋❋❋

Hours later, as Brooke lay sound asleep in Blain's arms, Mollie was five miles down the road, wide awake in her bed, watching a tossing and turning Freddy beside her. He was asleep, but the dream he was engulfed in was causing him to feel terribly unsettled. His skin was clammy, and his forehead was beading sweat.

Watching him, Mollie's thoughts went back to that night. The snow storm was worsening, the television news said the visibility out there was at zero. People in Breckenridge were advised to stay home, and be safe. Mollie had gotten all of her children to bed, and tried to call Freddy for the third time. He told her earlier he was working late, but would attempt to get home before the snow fall totals accumulated even more out there.

A few minutes after she put her phone down, Mollie received a text from Freddy. *On my way. Roads are horrible.* Mollie never responded, because she didn't want him to be distracted from driving. She was so relieved he was coming home.

Freddy was dreaming of that night again. He was driving too fast for the conditions of the road. The farther he got outside of town, the worst the roads were. They had not been plowed yet, but in his all-wheel drive truck, he was making it through. He had been able to see her taillights for miles, but then he lost her. She had given him an ultimatum. *Leave your wife to be with me, or I will tell her the truth and destroy your marriage.* Freddy had been caught up in a month-long affair with Dee Campbell. He met her at Ruby's bar on Main Street. He had never cheated on Mollie before, but he had thought about it. Wanted to. And finally, he had. Dee Campbell was exciting. She did things to him his wife shied away from in the bedroom. He craved this woman who had become his mistress. He knew she would be trouble for him, if he continued the affair, but he did so anyway.

Tonight, he had slept with her again, and when he told her he couldn't stay the night with her because he had to go home to take care of his family, she lost it. She threatened to tell his wife everything, as a ploy to keep him. They fought, and she stormed out of her apartment. Freddy got dressed and left after her. He really didn't care where she went until she called him and said her car stalled on the outskirts of town. He pinpointed her description of the area to be about a mile and a half from his house. He panicked. She intended to follow through with her threat to see Mollie, and tell her everything. He told her to stay put, he was on his way.

Freddy was en route to rescue her, but someone else had already gotten to her. Dee Campbell saw the headlights in her rearview mirror. She immediately stepped out of the car in the blustering snow. It was cold out there, but it was cold inside of her car, too, as it had stalled fifteen minutes ago. She saw a truck headed her way, and she assumed it was Freddy. As the truck moved closer and began to veer off the road, behind where she was parked, she noticed the truck was white and the man getting out of it was not Freddy. He was tall and lean with jet black hair and his long dress coat, dress pants, and dress shoes, were snow covered in a matter of seconds. She didn't recognize him as he approached. "You're in a dangerous spot, with that hill up there, I could have slid right into you! Are you stalled?" he asked her, appearing irritated.

"Yes, can you help me?" she asked, still planning to stay ahead of Freddy and expose his infidelity to his wife.

"I have jumper cables in my truck, but I'll need to move in front of yours," he told her, and she noticed headlights, behind him, which appeared suddenly at the top of the hill. The truck that was coming toward them was moving too fast. As the man said he would *be right back*, he turned around just as the truck lost control and slid sideways and incredibly fast down the hill. Dee Campbell screamed, *watch out*, and witnessed it all from the side of the road, standing close to her stalled car. The man walking to his truck, the man who stopped to help her, was struck by the vehicle. He never stood a chance. There was no time to move out of the way. Dee Campbell saw his body ricochet off the grill of the truck and then soar through the air, landing clear across the roadway. The truck spun another time before finally coming to a complete stop. This blue truck, she recognized. Freddy was behind the wheel, and responsible for hitting a man.

He got out of his truck, screaming and hollering in a total state of panic, and Dee Campbell hurried to his side, as they both made their way through the deep snow and over to the body lying on the road. Freddy was a doctor, and he knew instantly he had killed this man. When he turned his body over so he could see his face, there was considerable blood, but he still recognized Bryce Lanning.

Dee Campbell was beside herself, watching Freddy spring into action. He asked for her help, and she hesitated until he screamed at her. She somehow managed to help drag, lift, and carry, the body of a dead man. Freddy instructed her to help move the body into the flat bed of his truck. She felt sick to her stomach and asked him repeatedly why he was not calling the police for help. *I'm not going to prison* was his answer each time. She tried to tell him it was accident, but that fell on deaf ears.

With the body in the back of Freddy's truck, he maneuvered his truck in front of her car and managed to use jumper cables to get her car started again. "Go home. Leave now. And go straight home!" he ordered her.

She didn't know if her car could make it, but she was going to try. She knew Freddy wanted her to move her car as far away from the scene of the accident as possible. "But, what about his truck… and the body?" she asked him, trembling from fear and from what felt like Arctic air cutting through their bodies out there in the dark, where no cars had been by for well over an hour. The snow continued to pile up everywhere around them.

"His truck stays where it's at," Freddy replied. "Our tracks will be covered by snow out here in a matter of hours. Just go," he told her again.

"But, Freddy, the body!" she cried.

"Shut up!" he screamed at her. "I will figure this out."

After Dee Campbell managed to drive off through the snow, Freddy walked over to Bryce's truck and first now noticed the driver's side door was wide open. He had been so panicked, he hadn't noticed earlier. The truck's engine was still running, too. He left it as is. He didn't want to touch anything as he knew he would leave a trace. The blood from his gloves alone would be evidence.

Two and a half hours after he had texted Mollie, he finally arrived home. She met him in the garage. He was wet and frozen to his core. He had already removed his coat and gloves, which were somewhat bloody, and threw both in the back of the truck with the body.

"My God, what in the world happened to you?" Mollie asked him, pulling her pink terrycloth robe tighter around her as she tied a knot at her waistline and stood in her fluffy pink slippers only inches from him on the garage floor.

Freddy looked shaken, and that scared Mollie. Her husband, for as long as she's known and loved him, had it together. Sometimes his confidence in any situation even came across as arrogance. "Did something happen?" she asked him, again.

"Yes," he replied, and I need you to stand by me on this, just like we pledged on our wedding day, for better or for worse. And believe me, this is the worst I ever could have imagined." Mollie thought his face looked pale, and she noticed his hands were shaking. At first, she assumed he was freezing, but now she knew there was more. She had never seen him in this state of mind, and she instantly felt impatient being left hanging, but she waited for him to speak. "I was driving home and I got to the hill on the outskirts of Breck, I was almost home. The visibility was impossible and I started to lose control of my truck. I slid, I spun around, and by the time I managed to straighten out again, I hit someone." Freddy didn't mean another vehicle, but that was what Mollie had assumed. "I didn't see him, on the side of the road, standing there…" Freddy choked on a sob and Mollie covered her mouth with her hand.

"Oh dear God! You hit *someone*?" This was worse than Mollie had imagined, and it was about to become more terrifying than she could have ever foreseen.

"He was helping a stalled car, I swear I never saw him or anything until it was too late!" Freddy was adamant and he sounded like a child who was begging in desperation to convince someone, anyone, to believe him.

"Okay, I believe you. I do," Mollie said, still standing only inches away from him. He had not moved from the driver's side door of his truck after he closed it. "Is the person you hit…going to be alright?" She already knew what his answer would be, but she asked nonetheless because she was hoping with all of her being that Freddy had not taken someone's life.

"He's dead," Freddy answered almost too promptly, staring at her. He sounded callous, but Mollie realized he was in shock.

She inhaled a deep breath and the air in the cold garage burned as it reached her lungs. "The police know it was an accident right? I mean, come on, we are in the middle of a blizzard!"

"The police were never called," Freddy stated. "I couldn't. I can't, I won't, go to prison."

"It was an accident!" Mollie raised her voice at him, hoping her tone equivalent to shouting would snap some sense into him. She now had a thousand more questions for him.

"No one will believe that now," he muttered, "but, you, Mol, have to help me. Don't ever tell anyone what I did, or what

I'm about to do."

"You're scaring me!" Mollie replied abruptly.

"The man who's dead is Bryce Lanning," Freddy said, walking around to the back of his truck. His dress pants were soaked and mostly all snow-covered. His dress shirt and tie were wet, soiled, and wrinkled. He walked stiffly from feeling frozen, and Mollie stood there frozen from what she had just heard him say. Tears sprung to her eyes, "Brooke's Bryce? He's dead? And you expect me to keep this from her? Oh, Freddy, no, no, no! You're asking too much of me. She will need me, and I owe her my support, my love, my loyalty…and trust and honesty!"

"And that's more important to you than having a father around for our children?" Freddy was using the ultimate card. Mollie, like most mothers on earth, would do anything to protect her children from pain, or hardship, or sorrow.

"Don't you dare use them like that!" Mollie snapped at him.

"I'm sorry, but it's the truth. They need me, I need them, and if I get caught for this, I will rot in jail for the rest of my life." Just the image of him gone, away for years on end, locked up behind the bars of a cell, sent shock waves through her body.

"Okay!" she yelled, in an effort to shut him up and shut out the image in her mind. "Okay. I will keep your secret. I will betray my dearest friend in the world so you can keep your freedom. But, I'll resent you for this. I know I will. I can feel it. This is incredibly wrong. What did you do with his body?" The words coming from her mouth sickened her. She watched his eyes move to inside of the truck bed, and she was afraid, more afraid than she had ever been of anything in her life. But, she walked over to her husband, and looked into the back of his truck.

Freddy's coat was laying over Bryce's head and chest. The body, which was partially snow-covered, was in the back of Freddy's truck, in their garage. The moment was unreal. Mollie was shaking and she suddenly felt lightheaded and sick to her stomach. "I cannot believe you did this!" she yelled at him, and backed away from what she was seeing in order to regain her composure. "As if it isn't tragic enough how you struck and killed him, now you're going to try to cover up this crime? What in the hell are you planning to do with his body?"

"For now, we are going to bury it in the snow in our backyard. We're supposed to get another foot on top of what we already have out there tonight, so by morning it should be well-covered." And so would the road at the bottom of the hill, he thought.

"And when springtime comes and the snow melts? What then? Our kids play outside in that backyard. This is just too much, Freddy!" Mollie was beside herself. She felt as if she did not even know him anymore.

"We will worry about that when the time comes," Freddy told her, and then she stood there, watching him. He pulled Bryce's body by his ankles, and then pushed him off of the end of the truck bed and into the snowplow already attached to a four-wheeler. Freddy put his coat over the scrunched up body, opened the garage door, and started up the four-wheeler. Their house, on the outskirts of town, was the only house for a few miles. No neighbors or passerby would see him, and Freddy was confident of that as he drove the four-wheeler around to the back of the house with its headlights shining to lead the way. He placed the body in the snow and then used the plow to cover it. He buried the body deep with the existing foot or more of snow in the backyard, and he was counting on the forecasted foot of additional snow in the next several hours to pile on top.

When Freddy came inside, he was frozen solid. He went straight into a hot shower and Mollie waited for him in their bedroom. She watched him walk out of the bathroom, wearing navy blue pajama pants and a gray hooded sweatshirt. He sat down on the end of the bed to put on a pair of socks, in an effort to continue to try to warm up.

"You're so nonchalant," Mollie said to him, sitting in the chair in their dim-lit bedroom. "One would never know, by looking at you, what you just did."

"That's the whole point, Mollie!" he snapped at her.

"How did you drag that body around by yourself, alongside of the road?" There it was. The question he had hoped she would not ask.

"I managed," he replied.

"How? I saw you struggling in the garage." Mollie was insistent. "You said earlier that Bryce had been helping a stalled car. Who was out there tonight with you?"

"A woman who I can trust not to say anything," Freddy stated.

"Oh my God, Freddy! If that woman is half as shaken up as I am, she will talk to somebody. How do you know you can trust her?"

"I know her," Freddy replied, looking down at the ivory carpet in their bedroom. Mollie saw something on his face then. She recognized that look. It was guilt.

"From the hospital?" Mollie asked, hesitant to press him further, but she did anyway.

"No, from Ruby's. I've picked up dinner there a few times when I've been working late." He still had not made eye contact with her, and now she knew.

"You've slept with her, haven't you?" It had been months since he touched her, reached for her beside him at night in their bed. She thought he was tired, she knew she was exhausted from caring for babies all day long, but she never in a million years would have believed he was cheating on her. But, right now, after what she had seen him do in their garage, she knew. She knew Freddy Sawyer was capable of anything.

"No, that's crazy," he replied, and she was unconvinced.

Mollie started to cry, and he never moved from the edge of their bed. "You are a fucking liar! You're having an affair, and your lover helped you out there tonight on the side of the road!"

"Yes! Okay? Yes!" he reacted quickly to her sudden anger. "I have been sleeping with her."

Mollie got up abruptly from the chair. "You deserve to burn in hell, but I'll settle for seeing you rot in jail!" She picked up her cell phone from on top of the dresser along the wall, and Freddy stood up and darted toward her. He attempted to take her phone away, but she backed up and remained holding onto it in her hand.

"It's too late for that," he told her. "You are an accomplice now. I won't go down alone. Consider that before you make a stupid choice to call the police. Imagine our children as orphans…"

Mollie threw her phone as hard as she could at him, and it bounced off of his chest. She moved away from the sight of him and went into their master bathroom. She swiftly closed the door and ended up in front of the mirror inside the bathroom. She bent over the vanity and started to sob. She cried hard for the lives lost tonight. Bryce Lanning was someone her best friend loved. And her life, as she knew it, was over as well. Her children needed her. She had no other choice but to stay with him.

She didn't bother to muffle the sounds of her cries, and when she heard the bathroom door open, her face was wet with tears as she turned to find Freddy standing in the doorway, staring at her. He flipped the wall switch to turn on the air vent, which ensured no one else would hear her crying. Then, he backed out of the doorway and shut the door again. What a heartless man he was.

Mollie turned around again and looked at her reflection, and then she spoke to the woman in the mirror. "One day, you will pay for what you've done, you sorry son of a bitch."

As she lay there now, watching him sleep, Mollie had regrets. She regretted supporting him that awful night. If she had known he had a mistress, she would have never agreed to keep his secret and to help him hide the body. He had trapped her, and he knew it. That was his intention all along.

The body of Bryce Lanning remained hidden under the deep snow until springtime. Freddy kept covering it with more as the snow-covered yard began to melt in spots. There was a foot and a half pile of snow in one area of their yard up until May. That was when Freddy came up with a way to hide the body forever.

He surprised his children, and Mollie, with the news that they were getting a swimming pool. On their land, underneath the cemented, in-ground swimming pool in their backyard, was the body of a dead man. A man whose disappearance in the City of Breckenridge was thought, after all this time, to forever remain a mystery.

CHAPTER 18

Mollie was in the kitchen preparing toast and cereal for Alex, Avery, Anna, and Aiden. She was taking orders, who wanted peanut butter, who wanted butter, and what type of cereal, Cheerios or Corn Flakes? The two oldest children were in good moods as they talked about only having one more week of school left before their two-week Christmas break. Mollie smiled when four-year-old Anna asked her older siblings if pre-kindergarten gets a break, too? They told her yes, but to *enjoy how she only has half days of school now, because next school year she will be forced to go all day long, like them.*

Mollie ate a piece of buttered toast while she stood by the counter. She wanted to get out of the door on time this morning, because she had plans to drop off her two youngest at a daycare she had used before. Aiden would stay all day, and Anna would catch the school bus from there for the afternoon pre-kindergarten class. Mollie was wearing flared medium-washed jeans, a black ribbed turtle neck, and black clogs. She had her auburn curls down today and felt pretty as she had taken the time to get ready this morning. With four kids, she usually just threw on sweats, forgot about applying makeup, and left the house each day feeling like everyone was ready and put together, except for her.

She was feeling happy about getting out of the house today as she had plans to finish her Christmas shopping. She had ordered almost everything online and hid it all downstairs in one of the spare bedroom closets. When Mollie warned Freddy not to venture near that particular closet when any of the children were around him, he had gotten excited and promised her he would do all of the wrapping again this year. Sometimes, Mollie saw glimpses of the man she married, and once loved with all of her heart.

This morning was one of those times, too. She watched Freddy waltz into the kitchen in his dressy work attire. Eight-year-old Alex had a football on his lap at the table and when he saw his father, he gave him only a second to be ready for the throw. The two of them were tossing the football back and forth in the kitchen, while talking and laughing, and then Freddy playfully tackled his son to the floor after he had gotten up from table and ran around it. Mollie smiled at the other children giggling and she caught herself watching four sets of eyes on their father. They adored him. And, despite all that had happened, including how he had turned out to be a rotten husband, Freddy was a fun, loving father.

They all left the house at the same time, and once Mollie had everyone dropped off, she set out to cross the last several items off of this year's Christmas list.

While Mollie was at the La Cima Mall, she decided to stop at the food court for a club sandwich and a Coke. She checked her phone while she stood in line, to be sure she had not received any messages about her children. She enjoyed her time away from them, because that time was rare, but she thought of each of them and hoped they were all having a good day. Her children were her world.

After she ordered and paid for her food, Mollie found a secluded table to sit at alone. She unwrapped her sandwich and took a long sip of her Coke from a straw. She was looking down at her food and the handwritten shopping list she had made when she heard someone approaching behind her table. Mollie never looked up, assuming the person was just walking by. A moment later, a woman sat down at a table close by. She, too, was alone.

Mollie continued to mind her own business and she took a bite of her sandwich while she marked off two more items on the paper in front of her. When she did look up, she focused on the woman texting on her cell phone while she, too, drank a Coke from a straw. Mollie recognized her. She was well aware of what it felt like to know of someone, but not be a friend or even an acquaintance. Enemy number one was more like it. It was the first time in more than a year, since she had found out about her husband's affair, that she had come this close to Dee Campbell.

Of all places. Of all days. This was supposed to be a good day. It started out happy, and simply nice, and Mollie wanted to hold tight to that feeling. She forced herself to look back down. She had an appetite still, and she refrained from allowing *her* to ruin it. She had a successful morning shopping, and she planned to do a little browsing for herself before she left the mall today. First, she wanted to buy Freddy a gift from their children. She did so every year, as he did for her. Those were said to be gifts from their children. It would just be something he needed, like another tie for work, or maybe something more fun. That would depend on her mood after she got up from the table she was sitting at, only a few feet away from the woman her husband was sleeping with.

Mollie couldn't do it. She couldn't force herself to sit there, not that close, to a woman who had no rightful place in their family. Was it Dee Campbell's fault Mollie and Freddy's marriage had been over for more than a year? Probably not solely, Mollie knew, but still she felt sick to her stomach.

Mollie quickly crumbled up the wrapper she had spread out on the table. Her sandwich was only half eaten, but she had decided she really didn't want it anymore. She stood up, put her handbag on her shoulder and then picked up her two shopping bags, her Coke, and the trash from her lunch. Her movement caught Dee Campbell's attention and before Mollie could walk away, she found herself making direct eye contact with her husband's whore. And *the other woman* had the nerve to stand up, take three steps toward her, and speak.

"Hello, Mollie," she began. "How are you today?" Mollie sized her up in her ripped jeans which looked as if they had been painted on her body. Skin tight and accentuating her every curve. She was wearing a black leather bomber jacket, a low-cut emerald green sweater, and black high boots with large silver buckles on the sides.

"I'm fine," Mollie replied, suddenly feeling superior. *Who did she think she was?* Sure, Mollie may have carried thirty or thirty-five more pounds than this woman who was only a few years younger than her, but Mollie had class. Mollie was naturally prettier. Kinder. Richer. And, she was not a cheater. "I know this is awkward," Dee Campbell spoke again, and Mollie did all she could not to roll her eyes. Mollie knew Freddy had attempted to end his relationship with this woman. But, she had dangled the truth about Bryce Lanning's disappearance over his head. Mollie was not certain that Freddy had not cheated with other women, but knowing this woman was still in his life, and could be for the rest of forever, burned her. She was well aware of the secret that could destroy Freddy, and now all of them, because they were accomplices in the crime. Thinking about what Freddy had done, how she had agreed to go along with him to hide the truth from her best friend, and hide a man's body, sickened her. And, it always would.

Mollie started to walk away, but Dee Campbell stopped her. "You do know that, someday, he will leave you for me." Mollie stared at her. Her poker straight bleach blonde hair. Her inexpensive makeup, which was too dark for her skin tone and left a visible line underneath her chin.

"And what exactly do you have to offer him, aside from the obvious?" Mollie spoke with confidence. She even surprised herself with her own words just now. "He would have left you already if it hadn't been for your involvement that night." Mollie kept her words vague. They were in public. She never spoke of what happened to anyone but Freddy, and only when they were in the privacy of their own home.

"No, you're mistaken," Dee Campbell spoke up. "It's those kids who are keeping him from leaving." The way she said *those kids* unnerved Mollie.

"Leave my children out of this!" Mollie raised her voice, and suddenly didn't care if anyone had heard her.

"Oh, believe me, I'd love to," Dee Campbell sneered.

"I'm not going to stand here and allow you to insult my children," Mollie said, moving past her. Dee Campbell stood there and stared before she called out to her. Mollie never turned around, she just kept taking steps to move farther away. She did hear what Dee Campbell had said though, and it unnerved her. *Just enjoy them while you can. Life is short, you know.*

CHAPTER 19

Brooke's cabin was festive-looking. She and Blain had gone to a local tree farm and picked out and hauled off a ten-foot white pine tree. It was their first tree for the first Christmas they would spend together as a couple. Brooke left all of her ornaments from years past stored inside of a box in the closet. She wanted to start fresh with Blain. She wanted the tree they selected together to have new decorations and be theirs. She told him as much, and then he asked her to allow him to take the reins for decorating the tree. Blain insisted he had an eye for decorating at Christmas time, and Brooke believed him and agreed to leave the tree to him.

Two days before Christmas, that tree was still bare in the corner of her cabin. It had become a joke between them as Brooke continued to ask him what his plans were for their tree. He gave her the same answer each time. *I'm working on it.*

When Brooke walked into her cabin after work, she expected to see Blain because his powder blue Hummer was parked outside. What she had not expected was seeing her living room lit with only the lights on their Christmas tree. All white lights were strategically wrapped around the tree. An angel, made of all glass, was perched at the very top. And, there were multiple silver and gold bows placed on all of the branches. It was simple, yet elegant, and Brooke kept staring at the beautiful work Blain must have put so much time and effort into.

"I told you I could do it," Blain said, walking out of the kitchen in his faded jeans, fitted red flannel shirt, and thick white socks.

"It's amazing, so unbelievably beautiful, thank you." Brook had slipped out of her boots and she walked toward him in her dark-washed skinny jeans and high low white turtleneck. She stood on her tip toes in her black socks and wrapped her arms around his neck once she met him in the middle of the living room.

"I'm relieved that you love it," he told her, smoothing his hands over her bottom. She had started gaining weight and her body was showing some curve again. She kissed him full on the mouth and when they parted, he spoke again. "I've never been more excited about Christmas, well, except for maybe the time I wanted a bike and got it, when I was ten years old."

Brooke smiled at him. "Did Bryce get one too?" she asked, because it was easy for the two of them to talk about him.

"No, that was probably the year he wanted some dorky scientific calculator, or compound microscope," Blain responded, and they both laughed.

Brooke noticed he had the table set in the kitchen and she asked him if he cooked for them. "No, but I did the next best thing," he offered.

"Blain, I am really starting to pork out from Ruby's greasy cheeseburgers!" she scolded him and he laughed at her. He relished in seeing her look healthy again.

"No burgers this time," he began, "but we do have fillets, shrimp scampi, and a side of marinated vegetables over bow-tie pasta."

"My mouth is watering just hearing about it!" Brooke exclaimed as she grabbed his hand and pulled him into the kitchen. He told her to sit down when he donned oven mitts and carried their dinner from the oven, where he had been keeping their plates warm.

"What's the occasion?" she asked him, tasting the shrimp first.

"What do you mean?" he asked, nonchalantly. "We always dine in or carry out." She giggled at him. They did cook together, but not that often. "But, you're right," he spoke again. "We do have something to celebrate." Brooke looked at him with curious eyes as she kept eating. Blain had only taken one bite of his pasta. "My mother knows about us. I told her today, and she's very happy that I have you in my life. I told her I love you. I told her I've never loved a woman before, not the way I love you."

Brooke stopped eating and placed her fork down on her plate. Her eyes were teary and her heart had never felt so full. "She really is happy for us?"

"I think you already know she loves you. We talked about how she was afraid she would lose you, too, since Bryce is gone." Blain's eyes looked peaceful and happy and Brooke felt every bit of the same.

"I love your mother too, and us being out in the open is going to make Christmas so much easier than I thought it would be," Brooke admitted.

"Why? Because you cannot keep your hands off of me?" he teased her.

"That, too," she replied lifting her leg up underneath the table and caressing the inside of his upper thigh with her foot. He laughed at her as he sliced a piece of meat on his plate. "I'm assuming your dad knows, too?" Brooke asked him, and he shrugged his shoulders.

"He wasn't home at the time, but I'm sure my mother will tell him. I have no desire to share what's in my heart with my father," Blain admitted to her.

"I know," Brooke reassured him. "He's hard to reach. I get that."

"Bryce was the same way," Blain said, believing that about his brother.

"At times, yes," Brooke told him, "but I used to think I was meant to be with him because I could, most of the time, break through his walls." Blain nodded his head, and continued to eat. "With you, however, it's effortless," she smiled at him.

"I promise you, that will never change," he told her, reaching out to her. He caressed the side of her face with his hand.

After dinner, the two of them were lying on the red sectional together, and Brooke was staring up at their newly-decorated Christmas tree. "It's so beautiful," she said, still staring at it. Who knew you had such good taste?" she teased and he tickled her stomach. His hand was already underneath her sweater and he started to move it up higher to her chest. One touch, one kiss, one look. Any of it, always caused the two of them to end up making love. Blain's hand didn't get very far before Brooke sat straight up and spoke. "Why is there a red bow, buried in the center?"

"What?" Blain replied.

"You have all silver and gold bows on the tree, but I'm seeing a red one, right there…" she said, pointing her finger and then standing up to walk over to the tree. He acted as if she was crazy, and she was going to do more than just point it out to him. Blain watched her reach into the front of the tree, carefully lifting her arm up over the branches with lights and bows on them. And then she saw it. He watched her from behind, and he couldn't wait for her to turn around so he could see her face. In the middle of that sole red bow on their Christmas tree, was a knot and tucked neatly inside of that knot was a diamond ring.

When Blain's grandmother died when he was eighteen years old, she left him twenty-thousand dollars. He put that money in the bank, and promised his grandmother in heaven that he would save it to spend on something special. In this case, it was someone. He didn't spend the entire lump sum, but he did choose a beautiful princess cut, two and a half carat diamond ring.

Brooke's hand was shaking as she brought the bow close to her. She was in awe of the stone, the setting, and the way this man loved her. No one had ever made her feel this incredibly special. It wasn't just this moment, and the diamond. It was eating grilled cheese together at six-o'clock in the morning with tired eyes and bedhead. Moving through the snow-covered woods on the back of a snowmobile with him in the bitter cold temperatures. Riding shotgun beside him in the city's snow plow truck. Being in his arms by the fire. All of it was magical when they were together. And, now, Brooke was holding a symbol that Blain wanted to give to her to unite them in their love for each other forever.

She turned around, smiling through her tears. "What did you do?" They had become lovers after Thanksgiving and now it was only two days before Christmas, and he was proposing marriage to her.

"It's not what I did," he replied, standing up and walking over to her. "It's what you did, and what you continue to do for me. You make me want to be a better man. I don't want to spend a day of my life without you." Brooke watched him through her tears as he got down on one knee. She pulled the ends of the satin red bow apart and he cupped his hands together as it fell free from the knot. He held up the ring with two of his fingers. "I love you, and I want you to wear this ring. I want to call you my wife. I've never wanted anything, or anyone, more in my life. Marry me, Brooke Carey?"

Brooke whispered *yes* as she felt the tears free falling from her eyes and then she could taste them on her lips. Blain instantly stood up on his feet and wrapped his strong arms around her. They held each other so tightly before separating, and then Brooke looked down at the diamond on her finger. "I love it, almost as much as I love you."

CHAPTER 20

On the morning of Christmas Eve, Freddy was preparing to leave early for a few appointments at the hospital. He had promised his children and Mollie that he would meet them downtown at ten o'clock to take their annual family carriage ride and enjoy the festive music outside of the shops. Flanagan's Bakery had become their favorite stop on this day for hot chocolate and bakery goods. The large cinnamon rolls were the Sawyer children's favorite. It was their family's annual tradition, and Mollie was thinking about how Freddy never let them down each morning on Christmas Eve. She had not mentioned to him how she and Dee Campbell shared words at the mall just a week ago. But, since that day, Mollie felt empowered to hold her family together. She believed he didn't love that woman. He loved his family, especially his children. Mollie was lost in her thoughts as she stood in front of the mirror in their bathroom, readying to wash her face and brush her teeth. Just then, the door opened swiftly and Freddy came in.

"I thought you left?" she questioned him, making eye contact with him through the mirror as she stood there wearing only her bra and underwear. Neither matched. She had on a white bra and florescent pink cotton panties. She didn't feel sexy. She didn't feel embarrassed, or fat, or at all uncomfortable. There wasn't much to feel between her and her husband anymore. She did trust him to be a good father, and that was why she remained married to him. Thirteen and a half months ago, she chose to stand by him and keep his awful secret. She regretted her decision too many times to count, but each time she witnessed the love her children have for him, and he for them, she felt strangely at ease.

"My truck has a dead battery. I'm going to take your van," he told her, already holding her keys which she kept on the counter in the kitchen.

"What about meeting downtown at ten with the kids? How am I going to get them there?" Mollie didn't want to disappoint her children, and she too, looked forward to their tradition each year. They always had their family picture taken near the carriage, and at the start of each New Year, Mollie would send photo cards to all of their family and friends. They always looked happy in that element. It was the magic of the season. And those smiles on her children's faces were Mollie's purpose. In eight years, they had become her life.

"I will come back at nine-thirty and we will drive into town together," Freddy suggested, and Mollie nodded her head. He never said goodbye and she never offered one either. He just closed the door, and she resumed getting ready for the day.

Two minutes later, from upstairs, Mollie never heard the van's engine in the garage, but when Freddy turned the key in the ignition, the vehicle he was sitting behind the wheel of instantly went up in flames and the explosion took the entire three-car garage with it.

It was sharp and sudden, and just one really extremely loud bang, and then the noise of debris collapsing sounded like a heavy rain falling. Mollie froze as she stood in front of the mirror. *Freddy! Oh my God, the kids!* Her mind raced as she moved her body as fast as she could into her bedroom, shoving her legs back into her pink plaid pajama pants that were on the floor and then a gray hoodie of Freddy's that was lying on the end of their bed. He sometimes wore that while watching TV before bed. She was in the hallway before she completely had her head and arms inside of the sweatshirt. That's when eight-year-old Alex came barreling out of his bedroom. "Get the girls!" Mollie directed him and she ran into the baby's room. Aiden still slept in a crib and he was asleep as she hurried to swoop him up into her arms. She met Alex in the hallway, pushing the girls to move. They were both crying and clinging to each other. They had heard it, too. Apparently only a baby could sleep through an explosion of that caliber. Mollie raced all four of her kids down the stairs, telling them there was an explosion and she thinks it came from the garage. She led them out of the front door, directly into the snow-covered front yard. No one had shoes on. There was no time. Mollie was frantic that the house would explode next. All four children were in tears and freezing and none of them, including their mother, could have been prepared for what they saw next. Their immense, three-car garage, once attached to the house, was completely gone. There were strips and pieces of the siding, the garage doors, and even the brick scattered in the snow in the front yard. Mollie instructed her kids to stay in one place, and not to move, as they all stared at the ball of fire in what would have been the middle of their garage. Mollie couldn't see the van, but she knew it had exploded for some reason when Freddy started it up. It was as if her oldest son was reading her mind when he asked, "Mom, where's dad? Call him! Call 9-1-1!"

Mollie's first thought had been to get her children out of the house. She never took the time, wasted the seconds, to retrieve her phone, which was still charging on her nightstand next to her side of the bed. A split second later, they heard sirens. Someone had either seen or heard the explosion from the road that led to their house back in the woods. Mollie felt grateful when she saw a fire truck, ambulance, and police car tailing each other down their lane road. The fire would be put out. The house could be checked to ensure it was safe for her and her children to return to. Alone. She was the only one who knew that Freddy's life was lost. There was no way he could have survived an explosion like that, and Mollie's state of shock had not allowed her to even begin processing what that meant.

She huddled with her children in the front yard as the firemen raced to put out the fire. The chief made his way quickly over to them and divvyed blankets between them, telling them all to stand on one to keep their feet out of the snow. "Ma'am," the chief spoke, "is everyone out of the house?" Mollie nodded her head. "What about the garage? This looks like a car explosion. Was there someone in there at the time?" Mollie's eyes were wide as her three oldest children awaited her answer. She had no choice. She didn't want to tell them this way. *God, no.*

"My husband," she replied, her voice cracking, and the scene that followed was heartbreaking. The chief ran toward the firefighters to alert them that if they recovered a body, he needed time to get the children out of view. Mollie's heart went out to her three oldest children, eight, six, and four, as they cried for a man they would never see, and never again be a part of their lives. Their father lit up their world, and now he was gone. Mollie was strong and fought back her own tears, but she shared their pain as the paramedics helped all five of them into the back of the ambulance, to sit, warm up their bodies, and attempt to calm down. No one needed to be checked out, as they all had been far enough away from harm, safe in their beds upstairs, at the time of the car explosion in the garage which claimed Freddy's life.

It only took a few minutes before the fire was completely out, and Mollie watched the fire chief walk from the garage, toward the ambulance. She made eye contact with one of the paramedics, and she nodded her head. Mollie then moved two-year-old Aiden from her lap to sit between his sisters. "Watch your brother, sit close together. I will be right back." None of her children balked. They knew this situation was the most serious they would ever encounter in their childhood. They also knew the fireman headed their way was about to give their mother some very bad news about their daddy. Mollie had not given her children false hope. As much as they wanted to repeatedly hear her say, *Daddy will be alright,* they knew better. A male paramedic guided Mollie down from the back of the ambulance as her bare feet landed on the cold driveway. He shut the door then, and the fire chief met her right there. He told her a male's body was found in the vehicle, and her husband was dead.

CHAPTER 21

Blain heard the news first. He had gone into town for some pastries from Flanagan's Bakery. The downtown streets were bustling with people, as many attractions were taking place on the morning of Christmas Eve.

It wasn't eight o'clock yet and Blain was standing in a long line at the bakery when a friend of his from Ruby's came through the door. They wished each other a Merry Christmas and then Blain was asked if he had heard about the car explosion at the Sawyer home. Blain immediately said *no* and asked if anyone was hurt. And, he couldn't believe his ears when the guy replied, *Freddy's dead.*

✳✳✳

Brooke, in her white fleece robe, looked up from her second cup of coffee as she sat by the table in the kitchen. She had been staring down at the beautiful diamond she was now wearing on her left hand. The first thing she noticed was Blain had not been carrying a white paper bag from the bakery. She wondered if the crowd was too great and the pastries were sold out. She would have settled for a cinnamon roll, as she knew those were a favorite for Mollie and her family on this particular day each year.

"You're empty-handed," she said to Blain as he quickly removed his boots and coat by the door. And then she instantly recognized the look on his face. It wasn't a new look for her to notice on him. He looked pained. His eyes bore a sadness she remembered witnessing when Bryce first went missing and when the days, weeks, and months passed by with no leads and the unanswered questions remained.

"Something's happened, and it's bad," he began, and Brooke thought of his parents. "There was a car explosion, five miles from here. I'm surprised we never heard it, actually. It happened at the Sawyers."

"Mollie!" Brooke interjected and stood up from the table where she was seated.

"Mollie and the kids are okay, but Freddy is dead." Blain was not a man to tip-toe around getting straight to the point. He always spoke outright and then faced whatever he had to face in the moment. Brooke, however, sometimes needed a warning or a cushion to brace her fall. Her eyes widened and shockwaves recoiled throughout her body.

"You have got to be mistaken!" Blain walked over to her and stood close.

"I wish I was," Blain told her, honestly. "Get dressed, I will take you there."

✳✳✳

Tia heard her cell phone ringing in her sleep. Bo nudged her and told her to answer it. By the fourth ring, she opened her eyes and focused on her screen. When she saw it was Brooke who was calling her, she answered. Her voice was raspy from not having used it yet this morning.

Brooke never asked if she woke her, but she knew she did. She only said, "Mollie needs us. Get up, get dressed, and meet me at her house."

Tia interrupted her, as she sat upright in bed and Bo knew something was wrong as he watched and listened. "Tell me what happened first!" Tia insisted, and Brooke took a deep breath while Tia impatiently spoke again and asked her if Freddy left her.

"Freddy's car exploded in their garage this morning. He's dead." Brooke still could not believe the words she heard from Blain and now relayed to Tia.

Tia dropped the phone after telling Brooke she would *be right there!*

***

A rental all-wheel drive white mini-van had been delivered to the Sawyer's driveway. The police detectives on the scene had made urgent arrangements with a car dealership in Breckenridge. Mollie needed a vehicle for her children, as both of theirs had gone up in flames in the garage. The police were checking the house for more explosive devices while the paramedics were still keeping an eye on the children in the ambulance. They were told they would be going to a hotel with their mother for one night and could return to their home on Christmas Day. Mollie was racing through the bedrooms upstairs in the house, gathering clothes and belongings for all of them. Police were everywhere in her house. One detective even had a bomb dog with him, sniffing every corner in every room, on the main floor, all throughout the upstairs, and in the basement. She walked out of the front door, holding two large suitcases. One with clothes, and the other with toys and electronics.

As she stepped off of her front porch, she saw both Tia and Brooke rushing toward her. She dropped both suitcases on the ground at her feet and fell into their arms. The three of them stood on the hard, cold, snow-covered concrete in a huddle with tears. Mollie had not completely fallen apart yet. She couldn't. Her children needed her. The reality of this tragedy had yet to entirely sink in. It felt real now though, as she saw the looks on the faces of the two women who were like sisters to her.

Tears and tight hugs later, Mollie said she needed to get her children out of the ambulance and away from this scene. Tia and Brooke had driven the lane road at the same time and a police officer had stopped them both. They knew the Sawyer children were in the ambulance, and Blain, who had driven Brooke, had gone in there to check on them. "Where will you go?" Brooke asked, ready to offer her cabin. It would be cramped, but they would make it. Then, Tia offered, "Stay at my place."

"We are going to a hotel. We need time to talk and process this. I'm all they have now." Mollie's voice cracked, and at that moment she was scared. More scared than she had ever been in her entire life. She could handle raising and loving her children. She had done greater than her share of parenting the past eight years. But, now, she was spouseless and suddenly doubting herself and her ability to carry on.

"We're going with you," Brooke said adamantly, and Tia nodded her head. Both women were holding Mollie's hands. Before they parted, another police detective walked up to all of them, and focused on Mollie.

"Mrs. Sawyer," he began. "I know you're on your way out of here until tomorrow, but I'll need you to answer a few questions before you leave." Mollie nodded her head. She had no answers. Her husband left early for work, had a dead battery in his truck, and needed to borrow her van. He left. He turned the key in the ignition and everything blew. She wondered if his body was even intact. The thought made her shudder. Of course it was. The firemen found a man's body behind the wheel. They needed *a body* to say goodbye to. Her children needed closure. Her own thoughts felt eerie to her, but that's what she was being forced to think now. "The explosion that killed your husband was the result of a vehicle-borne improvised explosive device. A car bomb," he clarified, "which was activated when the engine was started." As the detective spoke, all three women stood there stunned.

"Oh my God!" Mollie said, covering her mouth with her hand, and both Tia and Brooke knew exactly what she was thinking. *That was her van.* Before the detective could question her whether or not Freddy had any enemies, Mollie blurted out. "He never drives my van, but his truck had a dead battery. That bomb was meant for me…and my children. Just a few hours later this morning, that would have been us in there. My children…" her voice trailed off, and then she spoke up quickly again. "How is that even possible? Who would want any of us dead?"

✽✽✽

Blain, Brooke, and Tia helped Mollie and her children settle into their hotel room. It wasn't anything special as most of the hotels in Breckenridge were completely booked for out-of-town travelers during the Christmas holiday. The three older kids were sitting and lying on the ends of both of the queen-sized beds, while the littlest had fallen asleep lying sideways across both of the pillows on one of the beds. The others were watching TV. Blain had gone a few blocks away to get them some breakfast. He remembered Brooke telling him they all loved the cinnamon rolls at Flanagan's Bakery, so he went there for a second time this morning.

Brooke and Tia were sitting with Mollie at a small, round table crammed in the corner with four chairs around it. "Thank Blain for me for going to get them something to eat, I don't think I did before he left," Mollie said, feeling confused and sounding lost.

"It's fine, Mol. He doesn't mind, not at all," Brooke told her, as she placed both of her hands, palms down, on the table top in front of her, and Tia immediately noticed her ring. It was not the time or place to mention it now, but Tia instantly realized Christmas had come early for her best friend. *Early* was the key word momentarily clouding her thoughts. It was entirely too *early* in their brand new relationship for Brooke to commit to Blain Lanning.

"Mollie," Tia spoke, shifting her focus to the crisis at hand. "What do think happened? Do you think the battery trouble in Freddy's truck was purposeful? Do you think someone wanted Freddy dead?" Tia kept her voice very low. The children seemed distracted by the TV, but she didn't want to risk them overhearing her. This tragedy had quickly become a homicide investigation.

"I suppose that's possible," she said, wanting to tell them so much, but she couldn't now. She could not talk about this with her children in the room. In addition, she would have to come clean with them. They would have to know how she had lied to them when they tried to tell her Freddy was having an affair. Just weeks ago, she acted as if she believed in her husband when for the past year she had not. That lie would lead to admitting her deceit. Right now, Mollie could not process how this could possibly play out with her best friends, or with the police detectives who would be questioning her again.

Dee Campbell's name would come up. It had to. She was the person Mollie suspected as being behind this. She didn't know exactly how or why, but Freddy was dead because of her. Mollie feared the car bomb was meant for her children, and her.

All she knew for certain was this woman was crazy. She wanted Freddy all to herself. She had admitted it directly to Mollie in the middle of the food court at the mall, just seven days ago. Dee Campbell's words echoed in Mollie's ears as she stared at her children on the hotel beds and then back at her best friends, who were waiting for her to tell them what she was thinking. *It's those kids who are keeping him from leaving. Just enjoy them while you can. Life is short, you know.*

CHAPTER 22

Mollie believed Christmas Day was going to be impossible to sift through. She tried her best to prepare her children before they left the hotel. She told them their daddy would want them to cry for him, and miss him, and wish that he was still with them. But, she also said he would want with all of his heart for them to be okay when the shock wears off and the pain isn't so excruciating. *Let's all promise to try to be happy, and when one of us feels sad, we need to be sure to be there for each other.* Mollie said those words to her children eight, six, four, and two years old. She wasn't even sure if any of them had grasped the finality of what happened yesterday. She wasn't sure if she had either.

When she drove on their lane road and up to their house in the woods, no one said a word in the van. All of their eyes were focused on their house, and the ruins of the garage. The debris had been cleared from the front yard, but there was police tape around stakes in the ground where the garage had been. The investigation was on-going. Just not today, as it was Christmas Day.

Mollie parked the rental van in front of their house. She asked her two oldest children to help her carry the suitcases and the diaper bag inside. She had Aiden on one hip and one suitcase in her other hand. She led her children up the front steps, and then stopped to set her suitcase down to free her hand to unlock the door.

When they walked in, everything seemed to be as they had left it. Nothing looked out of place, and even the floors appeared clean despite the foot traffic from having investigators on all levels of the house, after the explosion.

The kids just stood there after Mollie closed the door. "It's okay guys," she said, hoping her voice sounded confident and strong, because it sure as hell felt far from it. "You can play, watch TV, do what you normally do. I have the kitchen stocked and we'll make our favorite foods to eat all day today, okay?"

"Daddy likes chocolate chip cookies, make those for him." Mollie and her two oldest children looked at four-year-old Anna as she spoke.

"Anna," Mollie said softly, "I will bake those cookies, and we can all eat as many as we want, just like Daddy used to do. Okay, honey?"

It was a rough start, but after nearly two hours, Mollie was relieved to hear the TV on in the living room and see the electronics being charged on the kitchen counter. She had forgotten to grab the chargers when she was rushing through the house yesterday to pack for their overnight hotel stay.

While her two-year-old took a morning nap, Mollie was able to get the batter mixed for their cookies to bake later. She wanted to make a meal for lunch too, but she eliminated the idea of baking a ham with all the trimmings, like Freddy had enjoyed. Today was going to be different. Homemade pizza was on the menu now. As she was bent over and looking into the refrigerator, six-year-old Avery came up behind her. "Mom, you have to come downstairs right away!"

"What happened?" she asked, feeling alarmed. It was going to take time before any of them got back to feeling calm and unfretted about everything again.

"Santa came," she whispered, with an obvious excitement in her eyes. Mollie momentarily felt confused. She had told her children there had been too much commotion around their house yesterday and last night with police officers going in and out. She stated how she doubted Santa could even get in and out without being unnoticed. Then, she reassured them that Santa would come on Christmas night and they would be able to open their gifts one day late. Mollie knew she could not pull it off yesterday in time for Christmas Day. She didn't want to leave her children at the hotel, with someone else to watch them. She needed to be with them. Mollie had told Tia, Brooke, and Blain that she wasn't even certain Freddy had kept his word and wrapped all of the presents yet, which she left for him in one of the basement closets. Sometimes, he wrapped late on Christmas Eve after the children had gone to bed.

As Mollie stood looking at their 10-foot tall and five-foot round, decorated Christmas tree in the middle of the basement, she planned to ask her friends later how all of the gifts ended up wrapped and under the tree. She felt grateful to have such good friends. She appreciated their help. She could have pulled it off tonight, but she would have had to stay up all night long to be ready by morning.

When the baby woke up from his nap, Mollie brought all of her children back downstairs. They spent over an hour unwrapping gifts. There was surprise in their eyes and happiness on their faces. Mollie felt rejuvenated, and stronger, from all of it. They all missed Freddy, but they had managed to smile and laugh. The kids had a few homemade gifts for Mollie, and for Freddy, too. Mollie encouraged them through their tears to open the gifts meant for their daddy. It was painful, and they all cried, but they powered through the day together by leaning on each other.

By evening, they were joined by Tia, Bo, and Mac, as well as Brooke and Blain. Mollie hadn't expected them all at once, and she wondered about preparing a meal. She and the kids had not eaten anything but cookies and pizza all day and everyone was content with that.

Before she could mention that, Mollie watched Blain and Bo make a few trips back and forth from their vehicles outside. When she asked Brooke what they were doing, Brooke smiled at her and told her Blain had arranged to have a fried chicken meal catered from Ruby's. Mollie responded by giving Brooke a warm hug while she struggled to fight back her tears.

"Do I have Blain to thank for wrapping all of the gifts, too?" Mollie asked, standing close to Brooke.

"What? No. Everything was in the closet as you said it would be, and it was all wrapped and ready. Well, except for the mini training-wheel bike for Aiden. That was still in the box, and Blain insisted it's more fun to have bike ready to ride, maybe with just a bow on it, under the Christmas tree."

"Thank you," Mollie said, feeling her eyes well up with tears. Brooke thought she knew all too well why Mollie was on the verge of tears. It was blatantly clear, she assumed. Mollie had just lost her husband. But, she was mistaken. Yes, Mollie was heartbroken for her children's loss. But, her tears at the moment were for something else. Mollie was thinking how her friends, especially Brooke and Blain had put their holiday plans on hold to be there for her and her children. And what she had done to them during their time of sadness and grief was unforgiveable. She lied. She continued to deceive them. Now, Mollie wondered if she would she still be able to keep the truth from them when the investigation resumed after the holidays to uncover who was behind the car bomb which was planted in her minivan.

***

Mollie's children were asleep in their beds. Bo had taken Mac home. Blain was outside shoveling the sidewalks and driveway as two inches of snow had fallen on Christmas. Mollie told him it wasn't necessary for him to do it, but he insisted. He knew the three women, lifelong friends who supported each other through everything, needed some time to talk.

Brooke refilled all of their glasses with the Cabernet she brought along tonight. They were sitting around the kitchen table and Mollie mentioned again how she thought her kids truly ended up enjoying themselves today and tonight, despite the tragedy that just changed their lives.

"And what about your life?" Tia asked Mollie outright. "I know this is devastating for the kids. I get that. But, you, what about you? You have to feel, you have to allow yourself to grieve." Mollie only shook her head.

"Tia's right, Mol. We know how much Freddy meant to you," Brooke said, reaching across the table top for Mollie's hand.

"He was my world," Mollie spoke, "up until a little more than a year ago." Both Tia and Brooke shared the same look of confusion on their faces. "Freddy was cheating on me with the whore that hangs out at Ruby's."

"Dee Campbell!" Brooke interjected. "You've known all along? Why did you defend him when we brought this up just weeks ago?"

"I stayed for my children," Mollie replied, trying not to let on that there was more to this story. Much more. "He had a hold on me, I guess you could say. He was a damn good father, but he turned out to be a rotten husband. I loved what he brought to our children's lives when he was present in this house, but any love I had for him was gone."

Tia didn't want to ask, but she couldn't help herself. "Mol," she spoke, quietly. "Did you have that bomb placed to get rid of him?"

Brooke choked on her wine, and Mollie immediately responded. "God, no!"

"I'm sorry," Tia said, "I had to ask."

"You did not have to ask her that!" Brooke scolded Tia, and Mollie spoke again.

"It's okay, really, it's fine," she said. "I hated him for cheating on me. He was so open about it. I felt stuck, so I stayed. For my children," she tried to stress again.

"You and your kids will get through this," Brooke told her. "I cannot imagine your pain. I know from my own pain that I could barely take care of myself at times this last year since Bryce disappeared. I could not imagine having to keep it together for four kids."

"It's a good thing," Tia spoke, positively, as if she maybe was trying to redeem herself from making that last comment. "They will keep you going," she told Mollie. "They need you, and you are going to prove to yourself very quickly that you don't need a man like Freddy leading this family. He may have been a good father, but he wasn't a good man."

Brooke's eyes widened. She too never liked Freddy, but his family was grieving for him now. Brooke understood all too well what it felt like to miss and grieve for a man who didn't exemplify all good.

The three of them were silent for a few minutes as they drank together, and then the kitchen door, which used to lead into the house from the garage, opened. Blain had taken off his wet boots outside before he stepped onto the kitchen floor.

He felt as if he was interrupting something, and Mollie read that on his face. He wasn't sure how well-received he was yet with Brooke's friends. Blain started to back through the doorway again, but Mollie stopped him. "No, Blain, come in. Please. It's cold out there. Sit with us, Brooke will pour you a glass." Brooke smiled at Mollie, and then she noticed Tia had pulled out a chair next to her for him. This warmed Brooke's heart. Her friends were making an effort to make Blain feel welcome.

When he sat down, he looked as if he felt awkward, and he didn't say anything. He only listened as Mollie spoke to all of them. "I know who is to blame for this," she said, and they all sat up a little straighter in their chairs, and Blain rested his elbows on the tabletop in front of him. "Dee Campbell."

CHAPTER 23

On the twenty-sixth of December, Mollie was asked to meet with three investigators at the Breckenridge Police Department. Her parents had flown in from Illinois for Freddy's impending funeral, and to help her with the children for as long as she needed.

As she sat in the private office, her hands were clammy and she could feel her heart racing inside of her chest. This wasn't about her, she kept reminding herself. This wasn't about what she knew Freddy had done, and the secret she had kept for him. This was about accusing Dee Campbell. She deserved to face serious repercussions for trying to kill her family. The thought of her children, and the fact that they could have been in the van when it went up in flames, sent rage through Mollie. They would have been killed, if Freddy had not needed a vehicle that morning.

When Mollie drove downtown to the police station, she repeatedly thought of the same scenario. Each time she and her children loaded up and left home in the van, her eight-year-old son, Alex would sit in the front passenger seat. For a few months, he had been in a routine of helping Mollie put his siblings into the car. The six-year-old could buckle herself, the four-year-old needed her brother to help her sometimes, and the littlest always needed to be buckled in his car seat. Mollie would humor Alex. She allowed him to take the reins. His job was to load up his siblings into the van, open the garage door, and then turn the key into the ignition and start the heat to warm up the vehicle. *Only eight more years and I can drive,* he would tell her each time she came out of the house carrying the diaper bag. There was no way Dee Campbell could have known this, but Mollie would not have been the one to start up her van. It would have been all four of her children who were killed. Dee Campbell would have taken them, Mollie's entire life, from her in one explosive instant. It was obvious to Mollie that Dee Campbell wanted all of them gone so she could have Freddy exclusively to herself. But, Freddy's fate was sealed by a dead battery.

"What do you know about a woman named Dee Campbell?" one of the investigators asked Mollie, outright.

First, she looked surprised. Then, she realized this wasn't a movie, or a drama on TV, this was real life. People committed crimes, and were careless covering their tracks, and were caught by trained, skilled police officers. Mollie could not help but momentarily revert her thoughts to Bryce Lanning and how his body was never found. "She was my husband's mistress," Mollie admitted, without batting an eye.

"We have a man in custody. He was drunk on Christmas Eve at a bar downtown. He was talking too much. It seems he knows how to make homemade vehicle borne explosive devices. He ratted out a woman named Dee Campbell."

This was almost too easy. Mollie wasn't sure what they needed from her now. "Has she ever threatened your husband, you, or your family?" a second investigator asked.

"No, not that I know of," Mollie stated. "I only know she wanted my husband all to herself. She wanted me and my children out of the way. It was my van that exploded that day, and no one expected Freddy to be driving it." Mollie wondered if she should have said all of that. A part of her was very worried Dee Campbell would confess everything about the night Bryce Lanning went missing in an attempt to save herself, or in an effort to bring Mollie down with her. But, Mollie believed, if she was smart, she would not bring more charges against herself. If she implicated Mollie as an accomplice in Bryce Lanning's missing person's case, she would ultimately connect herself as well to that unsolved mystery.

"Are you willing to testify against her? Has she said anything to you, personally, that you could go on record with?" The three investigators awaited Mollie's answer. She pondered doing this, and then she thought of her children. She had to keep them safe from that crazy bitch.

"Nine days ago, I saw her at La Cima Mall. I had an encounter with her in the middle of the food court. She told me, in no uncertain terms, that if it weren't for my children, my husband would leave me for her. She ended our conversation with these exact words. *It's those kids who are keeping him from leaving. Just enjoy them while you can. Life is short, you know.*"

Mollie sighed after she told the truth. She wanted to get out of there, and not ever have to return. If anyone discovered she had the answers the police, in that very same building, had been seeking for over a year regarding the disappearance of Bryce Lanning, she would be sharing a prison cell with Dee Campbell.

***

"Dee Campbell is in custody for Freddy's murder," Blain told Brooke as she walked into the cabin and he was waiting for her, pacing in front of the fire he had already started in the fireplace.

"Yes, I heard," Brooke replied, shaking her head. "Mollie swears that explosion was meant for her children, not Freddy. And, she told the police exactly that."

"Dee Campbell will be lucky to be free before she's a shriveled up old maid," Blain stated, as Brooke sat down in the bend of the red sectional after removing her boots and coat by the door.

"Let's hope so," Brooke said, sighing. "This is just unreal. That woman is a walking nightmare who's affected all of our lives, Mollie's especially, in the worst way."

"I still can't believe she's capable of murder," Blain said, standing near the fireplace. "I don't understand what goes through people's minds. Who could even fathom killing children?"

"I know," Brooke sighed and agreed with him. "Her only focus was Freddy. She wanted him no matter what. She obviously never thought about getting caught. I guess most criminals don't. They must only focus on what they want, and they're blind to everything else, including the dire consequences when they get caught. And, eventually, everyone gets caught."

"Do they?" Blain asked her seriously. This had been on his mind all day long. Dee Campbell was capable of murder. What if there had been some truth to her recent outburst in Ruby's? What if she had killed someone before? The rumor was she had implied how she *owned* Freddy and had *a dead man to thank for it*. Blain didn't know what to think, but he was thinking about his brother.

"Bryce's case had always been labeled as a missing person, not a murder," she told him, choosing not to believe Freddy had anything to do with that.

"Remember how she acted here, in this cabin? We wrote her off that night because we were so angry that she had lied and forced a wedge between us, but think back, Brooke. Think about her words," Blain was adamant.

Brooke sat there before speaking, and then finally, she responded, "I don't know, something about *someone always seeing something, and do people really disappear entirely without a trace?* I just thought she was trying to get to us with more lies, you know?"

"Me, too," Blain told her, "but now I wonder what she really meant when she said, *sometimes no one comes along, and people are unfortunately left to fend for themselves and struggle for survival. Some never make it out alive.*"

"Jesus," Brooke responded, now looking at Dee Campbell as not only a lying whore, but a murderer. *She killed Freddy. Had she been involved in Bryce's disappearance too?*

***

The police spent three days building a solid case against Dee Campbell. They had the statement from the man who built the bomb and claimed to have sold it to Dee Campbell. He remained in custody. Mollie had gone on record with Dee Campbell's public statement to her about Freddy's children being the only thing keeping him from leaving his family. It wasn't a threat, but it could pass in court as foreshadowing a warning.

On the day of Freddy's funeral, Dee Campbell did not attend. She intended to, but she was arrested beforehand. In exchange for dropped charges, the bomb maker revealed proof to the police. Proof that Dee Campbell purchased the bomb from him and planted it inside of the minivan in the Sawyer's garage. The police weren't releasing him, and he got scared. He admitted how he had access to a video, which was not found when the police searched his apartment, computer, and cell phone. The incriminating video had been stored on his cell phone, but then deleted after he sent it to a close friend to protect for him. When the police obtained the video, they watched Dee Campbell enter an apartment and pay cash in exchange for the bomb. They heard her ask how to install it when she planted it, and she specified that she would be blowing up a minivan parked in a three-car garage on the outskirts of the city. The bomb maker was protecting himself. He had sold vehicle-borne improvised explosive devices before and had never gotten caught. He always documented the sale, as a precaution. In this case it was the insurance he needed to save himself from going to prison. Dee Campbell, on the other hand, was going to be locked up for a very long time for the murder of Freddy Sawyer.

***

The casket was closed. Mollie told Brooke and Tia before the memorial service that when she viewed Freddy's body, she was certain she did not want her children to remember him like that. He wasn't unrecognizable from the explosion, but he didn't look very much like himself either.

Brooke and Tia helped Mollie with her children while they were asked to stand by a closed, large, wooden box with their father's pictures displayed on top of it. There were a few framed pictures of Freddy with Mollie, a few of him alone, and all the rest were of him with his children. Mollie stood near the casket, as Brooke sat in a chair close to her as she held Aiden in her arms while he slept soundly on her lap. The other three children were at Mollie's side. It was draining for them to be there, to have to go through such pain and devastation, and it broke Brooke's heart to watch all of them. Tia had gotten a phone call and stepped out of the room for a few minutes. The two of them had not left Mollie's side for very long since the morning of Christmas Eve. They wanted to be her strength. She needed them and the comfort they brought to her and her children right now.

Brooke sat there thinking, *at least Mollie had closure. At least she knows under the lid of the casket lies her husband, a man she once loved.* If Bryce was dead, Brooke never faced closure. That was the worst part of knowing and loving someone who was in your life one day, and missing the next.

When Tia returned, her eyes were wide. She looked directly at Brooke and sat down beside her in the adjacent chair. She kept her voice to a whisper as she spoke to Mollie. "We don't have to worry about Dee Campbell showing up. She was arrested this morning. The charges are concrete."

"Did she confess?" Brooke asked, hoping for Mollie's sake that this woman would get life without parole.

"No. The bomb maker came forward with a tape. Bo said it was a sex tape because Dee Campbell could only afford half of the price of the bomb. Also recorded was her purchasing the bomb and asking specific questions about planting and installing it into a minivan."

"This is all unbelievable," Brooke whispered back. "Did this come from a credible source?"

Tia nodded her head and replied, "Blain. He tried calling you, but said you're not answering."

"My phone's on mute in my handbag," Brooke gestured to the floor, near her feet, beside her chair. "He'll be here after work. I'll talk to him then, but I'm glad he gave me the message through Bo, and you. My stomach has been in knots thinking Dee Campbell could walk through that door any minute. She's the last thing Mollie needs today."

"No chance of that," Tia said, as four-year-old Anna came up to her and crawled onto her lap. She was wearing a little navy blue velvet dress with a bow to match tied at the waistline. It was supposed to be her Christmas dress. Instead, she was wearing it at her daddy's funeral.

CHAPTER 24

On his lunch break, Blain walked into the Breckenridge Police Department. Detective Ty Clarke had been waiting for him.

"What's on your mind?" he asked Blain as he invited him into his small office, and closed the door behind them. It had been a few months since Blain had come to see him regarding any possible new leads on his brother's case.

"The unsolved mystery," he replied, referring to Bryce's disappearance. "As I've said, time and again, I'm sure you've covered all bases, and I know there hasn't been a single lead to chase down. Bryce seemed to have dropped off the face of the earth that night. But, a few weeks ago, something was said at Ruby's and now I wish I would have come to you with this sooner."

Ty Clarke nodded his head. "If I'm correct in assuming what you're talking about, that was brought to our attention and we followed up on it. The late Freddy Sawyer had an alibi that night."

"Dee Campbell isn't a credible alibi," Blain stated.

"No, she's not, but his wife is. Mollie Sawyer confirmed her husband's alibi. He was home in time for dinner, and safe and sound all night with his family."

Blain shook his head. "Fair enough," he said. "I've just been thinking if a woman like Dee Campbell was capable of blowing up a car to murder someone, then maybe her outburst at Ruby's had some truth to it."

"I agree," Ty Clarke said. "I wish we could provide some answers for you and Miss Carey." He wanted to add, *we're not giving up*, but those words just seemed stale after all this time.

***

"I really don't think Dee Campbell had anything to do with it," Brooke said to Blain while they ate bowls of chili on trays in front of the red sectional facing the fire in the fireplace. Blain had told her about his visit to the police station today. "I mean, given how she handled planting a bomb in Mollie's van shows you how ignorant she is. She couldn't be behind Bryce's disappearance. If that was a crime, it was flawless. Even the police have said there was zero evidence and not a single lead."

"So, maybe she knows something. Maybe something that came from Freddy?" Blain suggested.

"Freddy is dead," Brooke told him. "Not that I believe he had anything to do with it, but I think Mollie just needs to find peace and move on."

"I'll drop it, if you do one thing for me," Blain bargained. "Ask Mollie about that night. See if Freddy was home in time for dinner." Blain was serious. He wanted to know if Mollie lied to the police to cover for Freddy.

"It will seem strange to ask her that," Brooke stated.

"If it comes up, you know, in conversation about the night Bryce disappeared, just ask her." Brooke nonchalantly agreed, and Blain was content with leaving it at that.

✲✲✲

Six weeks had passed. Mollie and her children were gradually learning how to settle into a new life together, without Freddy. What pained Mollie most was witnessing what an extreme blow it was for her children to lose their father. Her oldest, Alex started to lose interest in playing sports. He used to love basketball and football for so many reasons, but especially because his dad did. His grades, which he used to strive for a B average, were hurting. Mollie gently warned him that if he didn't bring his grades up, he wouldn't be able to stay on the sports teams at school. Alex lashed out at her that night and told her he didn't care anymore. Not about anything. Mollie scheduled a meeting at school to try to help her son. She met with his teachers, two coaches, and the principal. They all had been aware of what the Sawyer kids were going through, but it was the twenty-two-year-old basketball coach who helped Mollie that day. He told her he lost his own father to a chronic illness when he was a year younger than Alex. He told Mollie that he recognized the similar stages of grief in Alex, and he asked her if it would be okay to keep Alex a half an hour longer after each basketball practice. They would talk, or maybe Alex would just listen. Mollie was beyond relieved to agree to that, and after two weeks, she had already noticed a positive difference in her son.

The girls were altogether different about dealing with losing their father. They cried a lot, and talked about how they were feeling. They were sad he was gone. They were mad at him for leaving them. Communication helped them to deal with their loss. Mollie did notice too how her daughters, Avery and Anna, who were only six and four, worked harder to please her. The girls attached themselves to her even more now that she was the only parent they had left. And, two-year-old Aiden was the most resilient. He loved whoever was present and taking care of him. He did ask, *where's daddy*, repeatedly at the same time each evening when he used to expect to see Freddy at home in time for dinner. But, lately, that question had begun to taper off.

Aside from feeling their pain and doing her damndest to help them all heal, Mollie was doing alright. She no longer felt trapped in a loveless marriage, or forced to pretend she supported a man she no longer trusted. The past six weeks, Mollie had proven to herself that she could handle being a single mother. For eight years, she parented mostly on her own anyway. She took care of their needs, their wants. She transported them to school and to their extracurricular activities. Freddy was always too busy to help. While his children believed he was working, Mollie knew that was not always the case. She would never tarnish their father's image in her children's eyes, especially now that he was gone. Freddy had been their provider, and the parent who was always fun. He never disciplined his children. That was Mollie's job. So much had been left up to her, which had now made the transition to life without him almost seamless.

There was just one thing Mollie knew she needed to change. And she wanted to do that for herself, and indirectly for her children too, as soon as possible.

Mollie had called the meeting, which was paraphrased as a *date night* among herself, Brooke, and Tia. They gathered at Brooke's cabin in mid February for dinner and drinks.

Mollie made rice pilaf, Tia brought Bo's famous Caesar salad, and Brooke had prepared baked Lobster tails. They were in the kitchen, all seated around the table, eating and drinking Cabernet. This hadn't been the first time they were together since the holidays as both Tia and Brooke made a point to check on Mollie and the kids at least weekly. Blain had even been back and forth more than a few times to help Mollie with snow removal, and once he had tweaked a problem with one of her garage doors after their three-car garage was reconstructed. Checking on Mollie had become a regular part of all of their lives. To each of them, she appeared to be managing exceptionally well. Brooke and Tia had even discussed privately how Mollie had changed since Freddy died. She was different. Better. Happier. Back to her old self.

"This dinner is amazing," Mollie said, taking a bite of lobster off of her fork and attempting to chew politely while she spoke.

"It is," Tia agreed and Brooke shook her head in agreement while she took a sip of her wine.

They had already talked about Mollie's kids, the continued success of Tia's business, and Blain. Brooke confessed to them how she and Blain were thinking of going to Vegas in the spring, to get married. Brooke was surprised by their same reactions. They wanted to be there. No matter where she said *I do* for the first time was entirely up to her, but her girlfriends wanted to be present. The mere thought of it warmed Brooke's heart. She knew it would touch Blain as well. He had come to really care about her friends, especially Mollie, the past couple of months.

Their party moved to the red sectional facing the fireplace. With refilled glasses of Cabernet in all of their hands, Mollie was giggling at something Tia said and Brooke just sat back and watched them together. The two women she loved most in this world. They had grown up together, all having met when they were eight years old. Now, twenty years later, they were still strong in their friendship and love for each other. Their road together, and their roads separately, had not always been smooth, but their friendship endured it all. Brooke was especially concentrating on Mollie's face. She looked radiant. Her frame was still chubbier than ever, but that was Mollie. She had the most beautiful facial features of all three of them. High cheek bones. Big brown eyes with naturally long and full lashes. She was wearing black semi-fitted jeans tonight with an oversized gold cowl neck sweater with sequins. Her long auburn curls were up high in a loose bun on her head. She had large gold hoop earrings hanging from her ears. She looked more put together than she had in years. She sipped Cabernet all evening and refilled her glass too many times to count. And, before, she always counted. She always left early to get home to her children. Sometimes, Freddy had called her home. Tonight, her children were with two caregivers at their house. Mollie had quickly grown to trust Alex's twenty-two-year-old basketball coach, Tim and his girlfriend, Darci. They had both become a go-to for Mollie when she needed an evening away. Mollie's parents had traveled back to Illinois after staying in Breckenridge for two weeks following the funeral. They had their own lives to resume. And, Mollie and her children needed to learn how to rely on each other. Tim and Darci were a godsend to Mollie. She knew she could relax when her children were in their hands. And, relaxing is exactly what she was doing tonight.

"You know, I've been thinking," Mollie began. "I need a job." Brooke and Tia looked at each other and then simultaneously at Mollie. They both knew this wasn't about money as they listened to Mollie explain. "Before you ask, no, I don't want to be a nurse again. I let my license expire years ago and somewhere in there I lost my passion for it. Besides, returning to that setting in Breckenridge would bring me in contact with too many of Freddy's peers."

"And that's a bad thing?" Tia interjected.

"I'm moving on from being the wife of Dr. Freddy Sawyer," Mollie replied confidently as she sipped more wine from her glass. "I don't know exactly what I need in terms of a career. I'm not, thank God, in need of a paycheck to make ends meet. Freddy knew how to plan for the future, and we are secure financially. I just want something for me. I want to be able to drive my kids to school and daycare, and maybe even pick them up, if there is a possible dream job such as that. I need to get out of the house, but I want to be in that house when they are looking for help with their homework or dinner on the table. All four of them are my life, but I realize how badly I need to feel useful without them, if that makes sense."

"It makes perfect sense," Brooke said, first. "I think it's a great idea, and maybe even something you should have done years ago."

"Freddy was against it," Mollie replied without hesitation. "He controlled so much of my life, especially in the last year. I feel pangs of guilt when I think about it, and now as I say it, but I'm happier being me without him."

"He cheated on you," Tia reminded her, as if she had to. "No woman should be expected to live like that. I know you love your children and you did it for your children, but now things have changed and I'm so proud of you for embracing this by recognizing it's time to do for you now."

"So where can we get you hired?" Brooke asked, smiling.

"I have zilch experience, but Alex tells me I'm a whiz with technology. He compliments me all of the time on how his friend's moms need help with all technical things. I'm the one who taught him how to surf the Internet, email, text, and even dabble with my Facebook and Instagram accounts. He and I have the same brain with that sort of thing. Freddy hated email, but we made him text." As Mollie was rambling, Tia was smiling.

"Have I mentioned my booming business has a website?" Tia asked, and Brooke's face lit up. Mollie, however, didn't want to assume anything too quickly. "We need help with it. We can't keep up with the reviews, both positive and negative at times. Our skincare is in all of the major department stores. The products are rated online on those sites so incredibly often. We need those reports. We need tallies. We need someone to sit in front of the computer, search endlessly, write reports, and brief us at our monthly meetings. I'm serious, Mol. This would be perfect for you. I don't have a title, but I'll drum one up. I don't have a set salary, but we can agree on something. You can work out of my office, or at home. You just need a computer in front of you."

"I don't know what to say!" Mollie exclaimed, leaning into Tia, who was sitting closest to her.

"Say you'll accept the damn job!" Tia replied, giggling as Brooke watched them in awe. She was in love with their bond, and the friendship they all had shared for two decades.

"I accept the damn job!" Mollie replied and they all laughed loudly in unison as they leaned into each other and shared a three-some hug. No one was the wiser to the fact that Tia had just now come up with the position at *Reality* for which Mollie would be perfect to fill.

There was much more laughing, and drinking, for two more hours. It was almost midnight when Blain opened the cabin door. He knew what he would be walking into before he even got in there. He could hear their laughter from his Hummer when he got out of it in the dark as the lights from the outside of the cabin shone on him.

Several weeks ago, Blain would have felt awkward, or even embarrassed, if he had come to Brooke's cabin and found them all there. Not now. Now, he felt like part of their group.

One of the family.

"Pardon my interruption, ladies," Blain said, removing his boots and coat by the door, "but a guy's gotta come home to sleep eventually. I see you're all still going strong though…"

They giggled again, and Brooke spoke. "Come on in, I'll pour you a glass."

"Oh no, I'm good," he replied, as she knew he had just come from playing pool and drinking beer at Ruby's.

"Come sit, and I'll tell you all about my new job," Mollie blurted out, a little too loudly, and Blain realized she was feeling the effects of the Cabernet he saw them all drinking.

"New job, huh?" Blain asked, walking over to the couch where three beautiful women all had eyes on him.

"Yep! I'm so shockingly good with computers that a multi-million dollar skincare business is banging on my door!" They all giggled, but again, Mollie roared with laughter.

"Well, I'm happy for you," Blain said, assuming he understood her right. She was going to be working for Tia. He sat down on the opposite right angle of the red sectional and Brooke got up to move to sit near him.

"You two are just beautiful people," Mollie said, slurring her words a little. "I mean, wow, look at how hot you both look together. I'm not sure I ever looked hot next to Freddy…"

"Oh come on, Mollie," Blain said, feeling like one of the gang. "You look hot solo, and you know it." Mollie giggled and Blain smiled, but she wasn't finished talking about Freddy. It was the alcohol taking full effect, combined with the desperate need to confess something that had chipped away at her soul for far too long. She didn't rethink it. She just started talking.

"He was nine years older than me, but apparently I wasn't young enough for him, as his mistress was three years younger than me." The last person any of them wanted to talk about tonight was Dee Campbell. She was still in the county jail, and bail was being withheld as she awaited her trial next month. No one had heard much about her, except for Mollie. She was summoned by the prosecution attorney to testify.

"That's in the past, Mol," Tia spoke, hoping to drop the subject suddenly at hand.

"Past," Mollie repeated. "We all have a past, or things we would like to leave there, and forget. Sometimes I can't turn it off, you know. My brain keeps wanting to relive that night." Mollie was speaking and everyone was listening. She drank the last of the Cabernet in her glass and wanted more, but she knew she had already had more than enough. "Freddy said he was on his way home, but hours went by. The roads were bad, I knew that. I just kept waiting for him to come home."

"Was this recently?" Blain asked, wondering if that was the latest snowstorm between the Thanksgiving and Christmas holidays. The first night he and Brooke spent together as lovers. Or, if this was *that* night. The night his brother disappeared. The suspicions he had before about Dee Campbell and even Freddy were now mounting.

"No, it was the previous year's blizzard. The night Bryce went missing," Mollie answered, and Blain's eyes widened. Brooke felt her own heartbeat quicken as she made eye contact with Tia. Tia wondered, too, where this was going. They all felt like Mollie had something important to say. She seemed so serious, and suddenly sober.

"Did Freddy ever make it home that night?" Blain asked, remembering Detective Ty Clarke telling him Freddy's wife had given him a solid alibi. *Home in time for dinner.* Brooke knew where Blain was going with this. He had wanted to know months ago if there was any connection with Freddy Sawyer and Dee Campbell to his brother's disappearance. He felt it deep down in his gut that the *dead man* spoken of in the heat of the moment at Ruby's that night was *his brother*. He was almost certain Dee Campbell knew something, and now, maybe, he would find out that Mollie did, too.

"Yes, late, but he did," Mollie sighed, and she looked as if she was speaking in a trance. She stared straight ahead at the fire, and continued to articulate her words in such a way which made them all feel as if she desperately needed to get something off of her chest. "He was frozen to his core. His clothes were a mess. He was a mess. I've never seen him so distraught, but yet so determined. Determined to hide what he did."

Brooke felt her hands shaking on her lap. She clasped them together, and wondered if she should say a quick prayer. Deep down, like Blain, she knew they were about to get some answers. And, yet, she was shocked at the idea that Mollie could have known something all along. Brooke couldn't take it anymore. She was allowing her mind to go somewhere that scared her. There was no possible way Mollie had kept a secret that dire from her. "Mollie, please. What are you getting at with all of this? Did Freddy know something about Bryce? Did Dee Campbell have something, anything, to do with Bryce disappearing that night?" Brooke was begging her, Tia felt frightened, and Bryce sat on the end of the red sectional feeling unusually calm. "Was he covering for her?" Brooke's voice sounded demanding, because she was desperate to know.

"She knows what happened, yes," Mollie said, knowing there was no turning back now. She had to tell them. She wanted to tell them everything. This had burdened her for far too long, and now that Freddy was gone she could confess his secret. But, it was her secret, too. She felt pained and hoped to God she would not lose her friends over her choice to remain loyal to Freddy. It was entirely about her children and keeping her family together, but would any of them understand her side of that now, after all this time had passed?

Mollie continued to confess. "Dee Campbell's car stalled on the outskirts of the city, at the bottom of the hill." They all knew the location. It's where Bryce's white truck was found. "Freddy was in a hurry, chasing after her I guess, I don't know and it doesn't matter. What mattered was there was someone who had stopped to help Dee Campbell on the side of the road. It was Bryce," Mollie stated, feeling the emotion of her words and how they instantly impacted Brooke and Blain, and even Tia, who were all beyond shocked and staring at her. "Freddy lost control of his truck, and hit Bryce. Killed him instantly, he told me." Brooke started to cry, and Blain put his arm around her shoulders. They knew. They now knew Bryce was dead. He was not missing. He was dead.

"What in the hell did those two do with my brother's body?" Blain demanded to know. Strangely, he didn't feel angry with Mollie at all. He just felt extreme hatred for the man she used to call her husband. Freddy Sawyer killed his brother, but worse, he covered up the accident that took his life. It was all finally coming to light.

"Freddy sent Dee Campbell home after he got her car running again," Mollie began, "Then, he came home with..."

"Oh my God..." Brooke said, covering her mouth with her hand and feeling as if she would be physically sick.

"I know, oh God, I know, Brooke..." Mollie sounded panicked. "I was in shock. I was scared. I was angry and I wanted to turn that son of a bitch into the police. I told him I would, but he used our children to keep me quiet. He didn't want to go to prison and leave them. I couldn't think, and before I knew it he was burying a body in the snow in our backyard. I felt trapped. I am so sorry! Please, you have to–"

"Sorry?" Brooke asked, standing up abruptly in front of the couch and charging over to Mollie, who remained seated. "Sorry for all the times I drowned in my grief, and damn near lost my mind worrying and wondering if Bryce was fucking out there somewhere? I needed that closure!" Brooke was screaming and crying at the same time. Tia was frozen in her spot, next to Mollie, and Blain never moved from his place either.

"I know, I know, I know," Mollie repeated, trying to calm Brooke as well as soothe herself.

"I can't take this, I cannot believe this. You are my friend, a sister to me for chrissakes! You knew all this time? How could you?" Brooke paused for a moment, and then she repeated, this time screaming, "Answer me! How could you?"

By now, all three women were in tears. Blain sat there with his head in his hands. He bent his body forward and ran his fingers through his hair and then just held his own head in both of his hands. He was thinking and trying to figure out where they go from here. First, he needed one final answer. He had been in that backyard a few times in recent months, and he had just now put it together.

"Mollie," Blain finally spoke. "What year did Freddy have that pool put in your backyard?" Brooke shook her head back and forth and Tia flew out of her seat, stood next to her, and wrapped her arms around her. They had been there more than a few times the previous summer, sunning poolside, and swimming in that pool.

"He made sure Bryce's body was under the snow until spring of that year," Mollie spoke, her voice shaking. "Then, he buried his body under the dirt, under the rock, and then came the concrete truck. Freddy was such a callous bastard about it. He told me the body was more than six feet under."

Brooke fell to her knees, crying harder, and Tia dropped to the floor, guiding her, holding her, and trying unsuccessfully to comfort her. Blain kept his face in his hands. No one was speaking, but, finally, he did.

"Who else knows about this? If it's just your late husband's whore, then how much does she know?" Blain asked, remaining calm from the end of the red sectional, while Mollie stayed seated in the bend, and Brooke and Tia were on the floor.

"Just Dee Campbell, but she doesn't know what Freddy did with the body." Talk of the body sickened Brooke. *The body* was Bryce. A man she loved. A man she mourned. A man who was killed and Mollie had known how and why and where and who.

"Are you sure he never told her?" Blain questioned Mollie.

"Yes, Freddy wasn't stupid," Mollie replied. "He said she knew too much the way it was."

"She could talk. She could try to get a lesser sentence for Freddy's murder," Blain spoke, feeling worried. He was sincerely worried for Mollie and her future. And, as Brooke watched him and listened to him, she wished she was half as compassionate as he was. She struggled intensely with her feelings for Mollie right now. And, at the moment, she really didn't care what happened to her. She had betrayed her trust in the worst possible way.

"I know that, but it could also backfire on her and she could spend the rest of her life in prison," Mollie stated, hoping that were true.

"She's going to make you pay for your part in it," Blain said. "That's the type of hateful person she is. Don't underestimate her revenge. You and your children were supposed to be in that van. She lost Freddy instead. I'm scared for you, Mollie."

"I know," Mollie cried openly again. "I can't leave my children. I'm all they have."

"I find it interesting that this nightmare, in your mind, is only about your children," Brooke spat at Mollie. "It was about your children the night you agreed to keep Freddy's god-awful secret. It was about keeping your children and their father together. And, now, it's about your children not losing their mother. What in the hell is wrong with you? A man lost his life!

A man's body was buried in secret in your backyard! How in the hell can you continue to live there? How can you live with yourself?" Brooke was screaming again, and this time she rose to her feet and rushed out of the room, down the hallway and into her bedroom. She slammed the door so hard the hinges rattled.

Tia started to go after her, and then she shifted her focus to Mollie. She obviously did not know where to turn. "Just let her go. Give her time," Blain spoke in reference to Brooke.

"Time to what? Come around? Forgive and forget?" Tia asked, wanting so badly not to take sides between her dearest friends in the world, but Mollie had just made that too damn hard.

"He was my brother," Blain spoke to them, "but he's gone, and so is Freddy. We have to protect Mollie now. She was an accomplice, yes, but a trapped one. Freddy knew exactly what he was doing. He deserved the fate he met. Dee Campbell deserves hers too. Mollie, you aren't like them. I know that, everyone of us in this cabin tonight knows that." Mollie was softly crying as Blain continued to speak. "We need to make a pact here tonight to protect you and your children," Blain said, as Tia gave in and nodded her head in agreement. There was no other choice. They had to stick together.

CHAPTER 25

Blain convinced Mollie to let Tia drive her home. He said he would make sure he brought her van to her by the time she and the kids woke up. It was already morning, going on one-thirty, when Blain locked the cabin door, put out the fire in the fireplace, and finally turned off all of the lights and walked back to Brooke's bedroom.

She was sitting on the end of the bed, holding a frame in her lap. She never looked up. She just kept staring at Bryce in the photograph. When Blain sat down next to her, she spoke to him. "I cannot explain how it feels to finally know what happened to him."

"You don't have to explain. I know," he said, "I've been living this, too."

"How could she?" Brooke asked, holding back the tears this time.

"It wasn't her fault. It was him. He made her. Focus on what a bastard he was. Focus on what you've told me about Mollie this last year. She was withdrawn. You always thought she was too into her children. It was her guilt. He did that to her. He gave her no other choice. She loves you, you know that. But, yes, she loves her children more, or at least differently. You and I cannot relate, yet," he paused. "We've only heard what it's like when you create a life and suddenly feel as if you would move heaven and earth to keep your child safe. She did what any good mother would have done in those dreadful circumstances."

"I'm too angry, and hurt, to think like you are right now," Brooke admitted, wondering how he did it. Bryce was his blood. How come she appeared to care more than Blain about what really happened to Bryce that night? He was dead all along. Brooke felt like she should have known. "You knew he was dead, didn't you?" she asked him.

"As time went on, I didn't think a man like him would stay away that long had he been alive. I think, deep down, I knew he would not have left you. You were his saving grace, or at least he wanted you to be. He was becoming my father, and I think he hated himself for that. I hated him for it, and probably do even more now that I know for certain he abused you."

"So you're relieved he's dead?" Brooke didn't want to, but she felt unnerved.

"No, but I am relieved to have found closure," he told her. "And, maybe, there is a small part of me who is glad he'll never come back to fight me for you."

"That's crazy," Brooke said to him.

"He would have been so angry if he had been here to see us together," Blain told her. They had not talked about this before.

"I loved him," Brooke said, sincerely. "Grieving for him nearly sucked the life out of me. But, you, you are different. You brought me back to life. I've never felt like this before. I want a life with you."

"Then focus on that," Blain said, smiling, and taking her hand. "Focus on the love in your life, Tia and Mollie included."

"She will be in irreversible trouble if Dee Campbell talks." Brooke was scared for Mollie. She was just so angry with her that she refused to recognize it. Until now.

"We have to come up with a way to make sure that never happens," Blain responded.

***

Mollie opened the blinds on the front windows inside of her house. She was awake early, after having slept very little. Her children were still asleep, and all she could think about was her confession last night. She didn't really regret finally revealing the truth to her friends. She wished though she had prepared them a little, and even herself. The alcohol was to blame. But, it was time she released the secret she had been forced to keep locked inside for so long. Now, she had to face the repercussions of being dishonest with Brooke. Tia had told her when she dropped her off last night that she wanted to help make things right between Brooke and her. She loved them both, and didn't want to see this terrible secret drive a permanent wedge between them.

Mollie spotted her van parked on the driveway when she looked out of the front window. Blain had said he would drive it over before she and her kids were awake. He was a good man, and Mollie would never forget how he supported her last night. She in no way expected that from him, considering he was Bryce's brother.

She continued to walk through the house, opening all of the blinds and when she reached the vertical ones on the French patio doors, she stopped, focused, and then felt her heart beat quicken. There she was, wearing her white down coat with gloves and boots to match. Her dark hair was hanging in loose curls over her coat's high collar and onto her shoulders. There was no patio furniture out there during the winter, if there had been it would be snow-covered. Mollie watched Brooke squat down and move her hand back and forth over the snow, near the east edge where the pool was located.

It took less than five minutes for Mollie to pull on her black snowsuit over top of her pajamas, and slip into her hot pink boots. She grabbed her coat to match, and then her gloves at the last minute when she left her bedroom. She made her way quickly down the stairs. She didn't know exactly what she was going to say to her, but she wanted to get outside, where Brooke was, and be with her.

Blain had driven his Hummer and Brooke had followed him in Mollie's van. After Brooke parked the van on the driveway, she asked Blain to come back for her in about thirty minutes. He hesitated, told her he didn't think it was a good idea. He knew she wanted to be in Mollie's backyard. He offered to go with her, but she asked to be alone. He told her to call him if she wanted him to come back for her sooner.

Mollie made her way out of the patio door, under the massive covered patio, and then out into the deep snow. There was at least a foot out there as they did not shovel the backyard at all. The kids played in it often and she could see their boot prints and three snowmen still standing from the last snow romp.

Brooke never looked up when Mollie walked toward her. She was upright and standing in the same spot she was in earlier, near the east side of the swimming pool. The pool cover was not visible, but it was evident where the snow had sunken in a bit in that forty-by-forty area of the backyard.

"It's cold out here," Mollie said to her when she reached her side. "You can come inside for a cup of coffee."

Brooke made no eye contact with her as she looked out at the trees on the far end of the backyard. It was all woods behind the Sawyer's house and the snow-covered trees looked like a breath-taking photograph made for a postcard. "I didn't come here for coffee," she told Mollie.

"I understand," Mollie responded, shoving her gloved hands deep into her coat pockets. Even with layers on, she was freezing out there. She probably needed more than flannel pajamas underneath her snowsuit and coat.

"Do you?" Brooke asked her. "Do you really understand what it feels like to know he's out here, maybe directly under my feet inside this cold ground as I stand right here, wondering what in the hell I should say to him? *I'm sorry you were killed? I don't like knowing you suffered pain when you were struck by a truck driven by my best friend's husband?* I just don't have the words, but yet I'm here."

"I love you, Brooke. I never meant to cause you more pain by making you worry and wonder about something I had the answers to. I felt as if I had no other choice…" Mollie's words tapered off. It meant something to her that Brooke was there. She had no idea where their friendship stood, or if they'd ever find their familiar closeness again, but she relished being with her right now. She wanted to help her heal, and she had hoped she finally gave her the closure to do so last night.

"I haven't stopped loving you, if that's what you're wondering," Brooke responded, still not looking at Mollie. "I came here to just be here. Now that I know, I felt drawn here."

"Do you want me to leave you alone?" Mollie asked, hoping Brooke didn't.

Brooke shook her head no. "I don't know what I want from you. I wish to God you would have broken free from that maniac husband of yours and told me the truth when it happened. I don't blame you though," her admission surprised Mollie. "I know how big you love. I know you were protecting your family, your children," Brooke admitted, as she and Mollie both had tears rolling down their cold, rosy cheeks. "I understand, but I am so angry with you."

Mollie nodded her head. "Scream, yell, push me around in the snow," Mollie begged her, "but please don't shut me out of your life. I need you so much." Brooke turned to her for the first time since she came outside. She pulled her close, almost roughly, by her hot pink coat, and then she held her tightly. And then even tighter. They both cried for awhile, and then Brooke let go first.

"Stay with me while I do this," she requested, and Mollie stood close to Brooke as she knelt down in the snow.

"Bryce," Brooke spoke outright. "I know the truth now…" she was speaking to the cold, snow-covered ground. It took her awhile to get the words out, as she thought carefully before she spoke. This was incredibly strange, but serene at the same time. "I'll pray that you have found peace. I spent a very long time in sorrow and grief, for you." Mollie was listening to Brooke's every word to Bryce. "I loved you, and a part of me always will. Rest easy. Goodbye now…" Brooke stood up and turned toward Mollie, and then she spoke to her. "I think I do want that cup of coffee. Make it a strong one." Mollie hooked her arm into Brooke's and the two of them sifted through the deep snow as they walked together through the backyard and then underneath the covered patio.

They were sitting at the kitchen table, just starting to drink their coffee when Brooke heard Blain's Hummer driving up the lane road to the house. "I have to let him know I'm in here," she said standing up. She opened the front door to Mollie's house and waved Blain inside. A few minutes later, he was removing his boots by the front door. Before he joined them in the kitchen, he walked through the massive living room with all pale yellow furniture including two sofas and three recliner chairs. Blain stood in front of the patio doors, and he stared out into the snow-covered backyard.

Brooke gave him a minute before she walked up behind him and stood close. "This is just so weird," he told her, scanning the area with his eyes through the glass doors. "I don't want to go out there, like you did. Not yet."

"That's okay," Brooke reassured him as he pulled her close and held her in front of the glass, looking out into the backyard and wondering exactly which part was Bryce's final resting place.

Mollie stayed in the kitchen and left the two of them alone. This continued to feel like a nightmare to her, and she hated causing her friends that kind of pain. When Blain and Brooke finally joined her in the kitchen, Blain didn't address the subject. He didn't blame Mollie.

"Kids still asleep?" Blain asked her, hoping to focus on something that made them all happy. Those four kids were special to him now, as well.

"Yes, they partied late last night, too," she answered with a smile.

"If you want, I can go get them something from the bakery for when they wake up?" Blain offered.

"No, but thank you. Blain, you've done enough and I know after last night you must think I haven't deserved any of it." Mollie poured him a cup of coffee at the counter and kept her back turned to him. He sat down next to Brooke, but he got up again and walked over to Mollie when she finished speaking. She looked at him, and felt teary doing so.

"What you didn't deserve was a husband who treated you the way Freddy did. He put you through emotional hell." Mollie let her tears loose, and Blain placed his hands on both of her shoulders. "That's over now. I promise you. I will protect you." He opened his arms and Mollie fell into them. Blain held her tightly as Brooke was watching them from the table with tears in her eyes. She only hoped Blain could keep his promise.

CHAPTER 26

Mollie, wearing wide-legged black dress pants with two-inch-block black heels and a white v-neck high low cashmere sweater, stepped up two steps and sat in the witness stand near the judge and in front of the jury. She looked out into the court room and tried not to focus on faces. It would only add to her nervous state. She did see Tia, Brooke, and Blain. Despite their efforts to wink, smile, or nod at her, she thought they all looked as tense as she felt.

Before looking down at her lap, she looked at Dee Campbell, sitting beside her lawyer. She was directly in front of Mollie. Mollie noticed how different she looked wearing an orange prison jumpsuit, fastened nearly all the way up to her neck. Her roots were showing vividly in her badly bleached, poker straight blonde hair. She wore little or no makeup and looked years older. Maybe jail time had done that to her, Mollie thought. She deserved to lose her freedom for planting a bomb with the intent to kill Mollie's children. Instead, Dee Campbell lost a man she believed she loved. *Karma*, Mollie thought, *came back to bite her in the ass. And let there be more of it.*

"Mrs. Mollie Sawyer," the bailiff spoke and abruptly caught her attention. He swore her in, and she surprisingly felt at ease. She had no intention of not telling the truth. She was not the one on trial here. Dee Campbell was the murderer.

The prosecution attorney spoke first. He kindly asked Mollie to tell the story, in her own words, about the morning of the explosion at her home. She did not cry, but she was visibly shaken as she recounted, moment by moment, the morning her family fell apart. The thought alone, if that had been her children who had gone up in flames, brought tears to Mollie's eyes as she spoke. She didn't have to, and she surprised herself when she did, but she spoke of Freddy as a loving father. She added how he would have wanted it this way. Had he known, he would have chosen to lose his life over losing his children. *He loved them that much*, she said. She was not looking out into the courtroom when she said those words, and so she never saw Dee Campbell wiping away tears from her own eyes. Even she knew how much Freddy adored his children. She was jealous of that love. That love was the reason she felt insanely driven to take drastic measures.

The prosecution attorney waited for Mollie to conclude her recollection before he asked her a series of questions. Had she known her husband was having an on-going affair? *Yes.* Did you know her? *I knew of her. I knew her name. I recognized her face.* Mollie purposely made direct eye contact with Dee Campbell during this part of her testimony. Had you ever met her face to face? *Once. In the mall.* Did she threaten you or your family? *"Yes, she told me in no uncertain terms that it was my children who were keeping Freddy from leaving our family for her. She told me to just enjoy them while I can, because life is short."* The attorney concluded his questions by looking at the judge and telling him he had no further questions for the witness.

Next, Mollie waited for the defense attorney to speak to her. She watched him lean in and whisper something to his client, and Dee Campbell nodded with a look of sheer confidence on her face. Again, Mollie reminded herself to stay calm as she was not the criminal here.

"Mrs. Sawyer, may I call you that?" Mollie nodded her head. "Despite the fact that your husband was having an ongoing affair with my client, would you say you and he were close?"

"We shared four children," Mollie answered vaguely.

"Did you love him?" The prosecution attorney interrupted with an objection that *Mollie Sawyer was not the woman on trial here.* The judge agreed, and instructed the attorney to get to his point.

"Assuming you loved your husband, would you say you would have done just about anything for him?"

"I don't understand the question," Mollie said, feeling nervous about where this was suddenly leading.

"If your husband asked you to keep a secret for him, would you?" the attorney rephrased his question. Mollie glanced at Dee Campbell and she smirked.

"That depends on the secret," Mollie answered.

"Why did you stay with your husband once you found out he had a mistress?"

"I told you, we have four children together. It was in their best interest that we remain a family. I know that for a fact now as I've spent the past three and a half months helping them through their grief for their father." Mollie remained strong in her answers and Tia, Brooke, and Blain were incredibly proud of her. They feared, however, that Dee Campbell may have confessed everything to her attorney.

When the defense attorney stated that he had no further questions, Mollie was surprised, and so was the rest of the courtroom. *That was all?* It seemed unfinished. He had gotten nowhere specific. Mollie had not been considered a key witness in this trial. That person was the bomb maker who had recorded the video of her. That was what incriminated Dee Campbell. Mollie's testimony, however, was what the prosecution was hoping to use to get to the heart of the jury. And he believed she did.

Mollie was dismissed from the witness stand and she walked right by Dee Campbell and her lawyer without making eye contact. She let out a deep breath as she sat down next to

Tia and both she and Brooke touched and squeezed her hand on her lap, which was clammy and shaky.

The bomb maker, who bore tattoos up and down both of his forearms, was called to the stand. He was a free man because he had helped the police catch the murderer. The courtroom listened to his answers to both attorneys and things were not looking good for Dee Campbell. It was evident that her lawyer would not save her from a lengthy sentence. The video shown to the courtroom clearly put the final seal on Dee Campbell's prison term. It was explicit. Dee Campbell ordered and purchased a bomb from the tattooed man who had taken the stand. She had specific questions. Questions, that, without a doubt, incriminated her in Freddy's murder. The video transitioned to a sex video and once the jury got the full effect of what had taken place in exchange for the bomb, the attorney stopped the video.

Mollie sat there in disgust. She was raised in a good, moral home. She married someone she believed shared much of that with her. How could Freddy, an upstanding doctor, turn to a trashy woman like Dee Campbell? Trash ruined their marriage, indirectly ended Bryce's life, and cost Freddy his own life as well. "Mollie, you okay?" Tia interrupted her thoughts.

Mollie nodded her head. "I just wish this was over," she said, looking at all three of them, and Blain assured her, "It will be soon." Mollie wanted to ask what they all thought of the defense attorney's testimony. *Did it worry them, too, or had she been reading too much into his questions?*

An hour and a half had passed in the courtroom. This trial was expected to only last a day, or two at the most, before the jury would be dismissed to discuss the case and eventually agree whether the accused was guilty or not guilty.

After the witnesses testified, the counsels prepared to make their final statements to the court. The prosecution went first. He summarized the evidence presented, and the relevant law and the arguments for finding the accused guilty. Next, the defense attorney in support of Dee Campbell was expected to issue his summary, but with closing arguments in favor of his client's innocence. He surprised the court and sent everyone out of order when he disrupted the protocol and called his client to the stand. No one expected Dee Campbell to testify on her own behalf, but she was about to.

Dee Campbell stared blankly out into the courtroom. She looked lost, as her attorney spoke to her. He asked her how long she had known and been involved with Freddy Sawyer. He asked her if she had wanted to kill him. She answered *eighteen months* and *no*.

"Explain to the jury what happened," her attorney instructed her.

"Temporary insanity, I suppose," she began. "I loved that man more than anything. But, I knew he loved his children, his family, more. I believed that if he lost them, he would run to me and want me as much as I wanted him."

"Did Freddy Sawyer trust you?" he asked her.

"Yes, I believe he did," she answered. "I had proven to him that I could keep a secret."

"A secret?" the attorney asked her, as Mollie felt her heart beat quicken, and she wasn't the only one feeling an internal panicked reaction. Tia, Brooke, and Blain were right there with her. It appeared as if Dee Campbell and her attorney were going to call out Freddy's crime in the middle of his own murder trial. And, then, Mollie, Tia, Brooke, and Blain feared the worst would happen. She would bring down Mollie with her.

They watched as Dee Campbell remained silent and again appearing extremely detached. Her attorney repeated his question, "Miss Campbell, you mentioned how you kept a secret for your lover. Please tell the jury what you meant by that..."

Everyone's eyes were on her, and everyone witnessed the color gradually draining from her face, her shoulders dropping, and her body taking a nose dive right off of the chair she was seated on. Dee Campbell fainted on the witness stand in the middle of her testimony. The courtroom erupted again, and the judge, the bailiff, and her attorney rushed to Dee Campbell's side. The judge spoke outright for a recess, stating the court would reconvene in approximately one hour.

The courtroom never emptied out though. Everyone was too curious what would happen to a woman accused of murder who had just fainted on the witness stand.

She appeared to come to after a few minutes of coaxing, but before she was helped out of the courtroom, Mollie, Tia, Brooke, and Blain left. They walked out into the lobby and found a quiet corner to stand in a close huddle and talk.

"What the hell just happened in there?" Blain asked, keeping his voice low. "Do you think she was prepared to tell all... and then lost her nerve and faked passing out?"

"That's what I thought, too," Tia spoke up and Brooke waited for Mollie to respond.

"She can still do it," Mollie said, panicked. "I was not expecting this. I don't know, I guess I should have been, but I didn't think she would want to risk sinking deeper into her crimes and give the jury further reason to want to fry her."

"Let's just hope they wrap this up after the judge reconvenes. Nothing went in her favor in there. No jury would take more than five seconds to find her guilty," Brooke said to all of them.

The four of them walked in the cold a few blocks down from the courthouse to eat lunch while they waited, but they made sure they were back inside the courthouse's lobby within an hour. And, just as the judge said, court was called back into session on time.

They found their same seats again, and watched the attorneys file into the courtroom, followed by the judge. Dee Campbell was not present this time. Mollie was watching the face of the defense attorney, and then she glanced at the judge. She couldn't quite put her finger on it, but something seemed off.

The judge called the courtroom to order, and then spoke. He explained briefly how it would no longer be necessary for the jury to reach a verdict. Miss Campbell was no longer on trial. She was checked by a doctor in a private exam room, and left alone briefly to rest following that exam. When the police guard outside of the door went inside of the room to escort Miss Campbell back into the courtroom, he found she had been a victim of self-inflicted asphyxiation. Her cause of death was suicide by hanging.

The judge never said, but Dee Campbell had acted quickly to tie the sheets on the gurney together and then loop them through the drop ceiling above her before she made a noose and slipped her head through it in a fast and dire effort to end her own life before she was caught and prevented from committing such a desperate act.

Mollie's eyes were wide. She could not believe it. Just like that, another life had ended. Dee Campbell was gone. She couldn't help but feel a relief like no other pulsating through her body. Dee Campbell died with the secret Freddy forced them both to keep.

"Let's get out of here," Blain stood up, and told the three women sitting with him and they all stood with him and moved quickly toward the door. They did not make it very far through the lobby when the defense attorney caught up with them. He had seen them leave, and he wouldn't allow it, until he had a word with Mollie.

"Mrs. Sawyer! May I speak with you privately?" he asked her.

"Privately is not necessary," she told him, wanting Tia, Brooke, and Blain to remain close to her. She was suddenly worried again that this was not over, after all.

"Fine," he responded. "I'll be brief. My client insisted she had a secret that would change the course of the case today. She never told me what it was, but she did say you were somehow involved." Mollie held a poker face, but she was shaking internally. "At this point, I'm well aware how it no longer matters, but I just wanted you to know that my client did have a heart. She was visibly moved by your testimony. The last words she said to me, before the doctor examined her and then left her alone, were *Freddy's children deserve to be happy. It's what he would have wanted.*"

"I agree," Mollie said, feeling disbelief that Dee Campbell didn't have the courage to face prison time, but at the same time she was bold enough to let go of hate and the prospect of getting revenge. In the end, in her last moments, she could not save herself, so she chose to save Freddy's children, and namely Mollie.

None of them spoke until they had filed into Blain's Hummer in the parking lot and closed the doors and themselves inside.

"Holy shit!" Tia blurted out, and the rest of them chimed in.

"Is this still the same day?" Brooke asked, buckling her seat belt in the front passenger seat and turning back to look at Mollie and Tia seated in captain chairs behind her. "So much happened in there in a matter of hours! Mollie, my God, you're safe from Freddy's awful secret."

Mollie had tears in her eyes. "I can't thank the three of you enough for being here for me. I never wanted to lie to any of you, I swear that's not who I am."

"We know that," Tia said, grabbing her hand. "Let's just move past all of the craziness now, please!"

Blain started up the vehicle and set the heat on high. It was freezing outside and it was going to take a few minutes for them to warm up inside the vehicle. He waited before backing out of the parking space, because he had something to say. He, like Brooke, turned to face the ladies in the backseat. "I know I probably don't have to say this," he began, "but I'm going to anyway, because I need to." They all waited for him to continue. "What happened stays between us. Tell no one. Not ever. We all just spent hours about to burst at the seams, knowing we were in the same room with someone who knew what really happened to Bryce. Forgive me, but I feel like we got a miracle in there today. Dee Campbell gave up because she didn't want to go to prison, but Mollie you were the one who was really set free. Take this chance, this new beginning, and live your life without that secret hanging over your head."

Mollie nodded repeatedly as he spoke to her. They all agreed with Blain. The truth about what happened to Bryce would stay between the four of them for the rest of their lives.

CHAPTER 27

"I just don't understand all of this," Bo Kenney said to his wife as they lay side by side in their king-sized bed with all white bedding. Bo was wearing black silk boxer shorts and Tia had slipped into a matching thin-strapped and very short nightie.

"It's a lot to process," Tia said, lying close beside him. Her long blonde hair was down in loose curls tonight.

"Mollie is just damn lucky Dee Campbell is no longer among the living," Bo said, still unable to believe everything his wife had told him. There were no secrets between them. "She could have been arrested and charged as an accomplice. I don't even want to think about what would've happened to her four kids."

"That's what we've all been saying all along," Tia said to him. "It's over now. That secret is dead and buried."

Bo chuckled a little before he asked Tia, "In the cemetery or under the swimming pool?"

"Stop it," she said, playfully slapping his bare chest with her hand while trying not to laugh with him. "No jokes. No talk of it at all. Hush. I promised I wouldn't say anything to anyone, but I had to tell you. You're my husband, and I don't keep things from you."

***

A few weeks had gone by and life resumed as normal for all of them. Brooke was sitting in her office downtown at her desk, punching the keys on her laptop when her cell phone interrupted her train of thought. She had received a text from Blain. It read, *Let's do dinner at Ruby's after work. Greasy cheeseburgers are on the menu.*

Brooke smiled, and replied, *I can't keep eating like that with you. My pants are getting tight.* She meant that, as she had gained ten pounds in the past few months. She knew she needed to, but the last thing she wanted to do was get carried away and get fat. She wanted to look fit and fabulous when she got married in just eight weeks. The date was set for the second week in April, and Vegas was their plan.

Blain's response was, *Then don't wear pants.* Brooke laughed out loud and sent him a final text, *See you at five-thirty. I'll be the one without pants.*

When Brooke walked into Ruby's, the dinner crowd was already in full swing. She looked around for Blain, knowing he was already there because she had parked next to his Hummer outside, and then she spotted him seated in a corner booth with a cute little blonde. She looked like she could have been in high school. They appeared to be in their own little world, talking with wide smiles on their faces, as Brooke walked up to them. Blain saw her and immediately greeted her, "Hi!" and he slid out of the booth and stood next to her. He put one arm around her lower waist and she did the same to him. "Brooke, this is Patricia," he spoke, smiling. "My little neighbor girl, all grown up. She's in town briefly from UCLA." Brooke felt at ease now. This girl was like a kid sister to Blain.

"Very nice to meet you," Brooke said, offering her hand.

"You, too," Patricia replied, "And congratulations on your engagement. I crushed on this guy most of my teenage years. You're a lucky woman, Brooke." Blain giggled. Flattery was something he was used to, and obviously enjoyed.

After a few more minutes of conversation, they parted from Patricia, preparing to get their own table for dinner. After they sat down, clear across the other side of the restaurant where there was an available table for two, Brooke was thinking about how Blain meshed well with everyone, even her friends had come to love him very quickly. She, however, did not know many of his friends and when she did meet them she felt like a square peg trying to fit into a round hole.

"It was good to see Patricia," he said, taking a drink of the Cabernet they had both ordered. "Her family was so great, growing up. I always wanted to live in their house, rather than my own crazy one."

Brooke smiled at him. She knew he didn't have the easiest childhood. His mother tried very hard though, and Blain would do anything for her. "Did she have a sexy older sister?" Brooke teased him.

"Actually, she did," Blain answered, "and we attempted the getting together thing, but it felt too platonic."

"Ahh," she responded. "She turned you down?"

"Pretty much," Blain giggled and Brooke took a sip of her Cabernet.

"I went to see my mom today," Blain offered. "I stopped by there on my lunch break. She was heading out for some volunteer work, but we talked for a little while first."

"Is she doing okay?" Brooke asked.

"I guess," he said. "She's excited about us getting married, but she would like to talk us out of eloping." Blain shook his head, appearing to shake off the notion that his mother already didn't approve of their choices.

"She and your father can join us," Brooke suggested again, and she meant it. Tia, Bo and Mac, as well as Mollie and her four children were all going to Vegas for their wedding.

"Are you kidding me? They never travel. My dad hates to." Blain rolled his eyes, and Brooke was quick to say, "Then just your mother should go!" Blain was just as quick to shake his head, and answer, "She would never…"

Blain's charbroiled cheeseburger arrived, along with Brooke's blackened salmon, and he still had his mother on his mind. "She brought up Bryce again, and now when she does I feel rotten for lying to her, but I know I have to. It's better this way."

"It's better for us in some ways because we finally know what happened, but for your mom there's still those *what ifs*. The wonder can eat a person alive. I know you remember as well as I do." Blain took a bite of his burger and Brooke thought he looked like a little boy with ketchup dripping off his chin.

"I do, but it is what it is. We're doing this for Mollie, and her children. I even thought about telling my mom, in confidence, that we know Bryce was struck and killed that night alongside of the road. But, then there's the Freddy saga and where's the body? Too many questions will come of it." Brooke could see Blain was torn about keeping his mother in the dark, consumed with worry and unanswered questions still.

"I'm sorry," she said to him. "I feel for you, and her, I really do. I'm not going to lie though, I am so relieved that it's over."

"Me too," Blain agreed, finally taking a break from eating his burger to wipe off the ketchup on his chin with a napkin. "Let's focus on us and putting the past behind us. I cannot wait to make you my wife."

Brooke smiled big at him. "So what will happen to all the women in waiting when I'm Mrs. Lanning?" she teased, and saying *Mrs. Lanning* aloud sounded odd to her. It was going to take some getting used to. She had been Brooke Carey for twenty-eight years. When she was with Bryce, she assumed one day she would become Brooke Lanning, and now it was really going to happen.

"They'll be waiting a long damn time, because I've chosen the woman I want to spend the rest of my life with." Blain was being honest, and Brooke was flattered.

"I'm her. I'm that incredibly lucky woman," she said, smiling and her eyes were lit, "but I still don't know why? You could have a Patricia or the next sassy, sexy broad that walks in here with her boobs hanging out."

Blain laughed at her. "I don't want anyone else, and your pleasure pillows suit me just fine," he said, winking at her and she laughed out loud. "And, let the record show that I'm the lucky one."

It didn't take much for the two of them to be happy. They only needed each other. They were opposites in just as many ways as they were alike, but for them it was a magical combination.

***

Bo was lying flat on his back in the middle of the living room floor, staring up at the twenty-two-foot ceiling. He was in excruciating pain when Tia came through the front door with a prescription of Vicodin for him.

Giving it time, resting, and doing the type of exercises, he as a physical therapist taught his patients every day, was just not helping. A dislocated disk in his lower back happened quickly and unexpectedly when he lifted a young boy during therapy yesterday.

Tia retrieved a bottle of water from the stainless steel refrigerator in the kitchen, rushed back into the living room as she opened it for him, and then handed it to him along with one tablet of three-hundred milligrams of Vicodin.

"Ugh, you know how I feel about taking medication," Bo grumbled, and then winced from the pain of moving to an upright position on the floor.

"Just take it! Jesus, I've never seen you in so much pain." Tia was concerned about him, but somewhat unnerved because he had pulled her out of an important meeting to send her to the pharmacy. Last night, when she wanted to get the prescription filled for him, he refused. The pain obviously had gotten to him.

It took two weeks for the pain to completely subside. Bo was able to avoid surgery by committing himself to do what he knew best. He was determined to get well by use of physical therapy. He implemented specific exercises into his daily routine, at work and at home. The exercises did not directly alter the herniated disc in his back, but he was able to stabilize his spine muscles and no longer feel pain. Still, Bo continued to take the Vicodin. Now, it had nothing to do with chasing away the pain, and everything to do with dependence.

It was eight weeks later and Tia no longer recognized the man she called her husband. If he didn't have Vicodin in his system every five hours, he became moody, disconnected, and he had abnormal shifts in his energy levels. Bo was dependent on that drug and unrecognizable to his family, his co-workers, and his friends.

Most recently, Tia discovered Bo had obtained a second prescription for Vicodin. He had seen a new physician, this one outside of Breckenridge and in the City of Dillon. He had gone to extreme lengths in his quest to get his hands on another prescription at a separate pharmacy. That drug had become his top priority.

Tia had packed a suitcase for herself, and one for Mac. They were flying out to Vegas tonight, with everyone except for Bo. She had stopped making excuses for him weeks ago. Tia was in tears and at a loss for what to do next when she confided in both Mollie and Brooke how Bo had quickly and crazily become a drug addict. They discussed sending Bo to rehab. They also questioned if Tia would leave him. *Maybe tough love would scare some sense into him?* Tia said she didn't know what she would do, but what terrified her most was that Mac was not biologically hers. She raised him, and more than anything she wanted to remain a family with Bo and the son they considered to be theirs. She had not spoken to an attorney about her rights, but Tia knew if Bo forced her hand, she could prove him to be unfit to have any type of custody of Mac. Things had gotten that bad for him. He was out of control.

Tia and Mac left the house before Bo came home from work. She reminded him last night that they would be in Vegas all weekend for Blain and Brooke's wedding. He had no response. The old Bo would have wanted to go, and be a witness to the wedding. Now, he was fueled by a powerful drug, and nothing else seemed to matter to him.

All nine of them were seated in the airport early, forty-five minutes before they were able to board their flight to Vegas. Mollie had taken her four kids and Mac to get some pizza by the slice and they had just returned with their bellies full. Blain and Brooke had already had a drink at the bar and wanted to wait to eat a late dinner in Vegas. Tia was just not hungry. She looked at her phone twice in less than five minutes, and Brooke noticed but didn't want to ask her anything in front of the children. She could see the stress and worry in Tia's eyes. Life with Bo had become unbearable. Brooke knew how badly Tia wanted to help him, but he didn't want to be helped. He couldn't be reached. Addiction was unfamiliar to Tia. She only saw it as selfish. And, now, Bo's choices were destroying their lives.

They were in line to board the plane when Tia reached for her ringing phone that she had put away in her handbag to free her hands to help Mollie keep a close eye on her children and hold a couple of little hands.

She noticed it was Bo's office number and wondered why he was not calling from his cell phone. She said *hello*, and a strange voice spoke in urgency on the opposite end. "Mrs. Kenny! This is Carter, I work with Bo. He needs you. He blacked out at the office, and we've called an ambulance. Can you meet us at the hospital right away?"

Not another word needed to be said. Tia knew she could not get on that plane. "Bo needs me," she said, frantically. "He's being taken by ambulance to the hospital. He blacked out at work."

Brooke looked at Blain and no words needed to be spoken between them. They wanted to get married. They would get married, but just not this weekend in Vegas. Tia tried to object, but she couldn't. She needed them, and they were going to be there for her.

Blain handled retrieving all of their luggage before the plane took off. Mollie drove her children and Mac to her house and she had called Tim and Darci to meet her there to watch them tonight so she could go to the hospital. Brooke drove Tia to the hospital.

"How bad is it?" Brooke asked her outright as she drove over the speed limit on Interstate 70.

"I don't know," Tia answered, looking straight ahead at the road in front of her. She was always confident about where she was headed. She knew when she looked in the mirror, she was going to like what she saw. She knew when she opened her own business, and later developed a skincare line, that she was going to be successful. Tia was not accustomed to failure and uncertainty. Now, in just a couple of months, she had been forced into that world. And she no longer wanted to be a part of it. But, her greatest fear as Brooke took the exit ramp leading to the hospital, was that Bo would not survive.

They were told to have a seat in the waiting area. They were lucky to find two chairs left, as it was terribly busy. Thirty-five minutes later, the nurse called Tia back up to the window. Bo was admitted and they could see him now.

Brooke walked with Tia to the far end of the hallway on the main floor, and they found him in room one-eleven. They walked passed an empty bed and clear across the room on the other side of the half-closed white curtain with a strange pale blue swirled pattern on it. Bo was awake and sitting up in bed, and a doctor was in the room with him.

"I'm his wife," Tia said, making eye contact with the doctor and ignoring Bo once she had taken a look at him and felt relieved to see for herself that he was alive. Her anger toward him resurfaced again. That's the way it worked lately. He continued to bring this craziness into their lives. *Unnecessary*, Tia thought. Again, she didn't understand addiction. And, she didn't identify with how or why he had fallen victim to it.

Tia and Brooke stood by Bo's beside. He, at one point when the doctor was speaking, laid his head back and closed his eyes. The doctor made no effort to spare Bo's feelings. The middle-aged heavy set man with a full head of dark brown hair stood there in his white lab coat with a stethoscope wrapped around the back of his neck and shoulders. "Your husband blacked out from taking his prescription Vicodin. I'm not going to say he overdosed, but he is taking this drug too often for his back pain, and tonight that caught up with him." Tia immediately realized Bo had lied to the doctor. He was no longer experiencing back pain. He told her himself that the physical therapy had worked. Now, he just craved the drug. "My suggestion is for Bo to check into a rehab facility to wean his body off of Vicodin." *So this doctor did know*, Tia thought. Of course he knew. The signs were all there. Bo's eating habits had changed. He never finished a meal anymore. He no longer focused on working out either. His body was visibly thinner, less buff and bulky. His nose ran often, and his eyes were red and glazed. "It does not have to be for six or eight weeks long. Maybe just half of that time? That will depend on Bo's mind over matter. If, he cooperates."

"I'm not going," Bo interjected, still lying back in bed with his eyes closed. The doctor looked directly at Tia. "He will be released in the morning. Might be a rough night as withdrawals will begin. If you can, get him to rehab." The doctor walked out of the room and Brooke told Tia she would leave her and Bo alone, to talk. The seriousness of Bo's addiction had come to light and it was time someone tried to force him to see what he was doing to himself, and to those he loved.

When they were alone, Tia walked closer to the bed and right up to Bo's side. "Open your eyes," she said to him, calmly. He did, and he looked at her as well.

"Do you have back pain?" she asked him.

"No," he answered her. "I've told you before, I just need that drug to feel normal."

"And I've told you before, I don't understand," Tia said. "If you're not taking the pills for pain anymore, why do you feel so dependent on them? You have always been the most cautious person when it comes to drug dependency. You never even took an ibuprofen for a headache!"

"I know," Bo agreed with her. "This scares me sometimes," he admitted and for the first time in months, she felt sorry for him.

"Then do something about it. Take the necessary steps to rid your body of needing that poison." Tia hoped she was finally getting through to him. The door was open so she walked up to the ugly curtain which divided the room and she pulled it closed so they could have some privacy from the hallway traffic which produced occasional onlookers. "Make up your mind to get well," she began again.

"I'm not checking myself into rehab," he said, again.

"You can't do it alone," she told him. "You heard the doctor, you may not have to be in there for very long. Just get the help you're going to need to fight the addiction."

Bo was already feeling agitated. His muscles were achy and he felt sweaty. Those were the feelings which had come on strong when he tried to quit the Vicodin a few times before on his own. "Just go home, and come back for me in the morning," he told her, sounding irritated.

"I'm not bringing you home," Tia said, adamantly. "I am not bringing you back into my life, or Mac's, until you are clean." Her own words scared her. This was the tough love she had heard about that other people felt forced to use on their loved ones with serious addictions. She didn't want to lose him, but the man she had been living with the past couple of months was not the man she loved.

Bo stared at her before he responded. He didn't look well, and she could see the anger mounting in his eyes. She had given him an ultimatum. The door to his hospital room was still open and Brooke could hear voices coming from out in the hallway. The hospital bed on the opposite side of the curtain was needed in another area of the hospital. She paid no attention to what they were talking about. This conversation between her and her husband was dire. She was done, and he knew it. The staff was swamped with patients coming in, and two to a room was a necessity. A volunteer was sent in the direction of room one-eleven to retrieve the extra bed in Bo's current hospital room. The beds were full in the emergency room and one patient who had been admitted needed to be moved. That volunteer was told to roll the bed out of one-eleven and down to the emergency room. She would then have to transport the patient back. The volunteer was en route to get the vacant bed when Bo and Tia's conversation escalated to an emotional high.

"Think long and hard before you kick me out," Bo warned her as the sweat began to bead on his forehead and his hands at his sides became shaky. He was sitting upright in bed and Tia was standing above him, glaring down at him. She immediately worried that he was going to play the card of his son not being biologically hers. "I'll talk. I'll help the men in blue at the Breckenridge Police Department solve the mystery that's been lingering in this city." Tia's eyes widened. Yes, she had confided in her husband. That's when she trusted and loved him above anyone else. Now, she didn't know who he was anymore, she was certain she didn't trust him, and she couldn't even find it in her heart to like him anymore. "Your best friend will go to jail. She'll lose her children."

"Stop it! Stop it right now!" Tia raised her voice. "Who are you? You're trying to blackmail me now? You're no better than Freddy Sawyer, you son of a bitch!"

Bo shot back at her with more hateful words. "If I hit a man with my truck, I wouldn't bury his body in my own backyard under the cement from my swimming pool!" he defended himself.

The two of them were so angry with each other. Behind that pulled curtain which divided the hospital room, they were swapping hurtful words and serious threats. They had not paid attention, they were oblivious to the fact that on the opposite side of the room stood a hospital volunteer who had heard Bo's every word. Julie Lanning had been a hospital volunteer for the past ten years. She knew what she heard. She made no mistake. She was certain and shocked and reeling from finally knowing what happened to her son. *He was struck by a vehicle. He was dead. He was buried. He was dead. Dead…Dead…Dead…*

Those words rang in her ears. Over and over. And then she felt the room begin to spin. She stumbled backwards, finding it more difficult to walk with each step. Her heart was beating so fast, her head hurt. It was a piercing pain. She made her way out of the room, unheard, and as soon as she entered the hallway she fell back, up against the wall. She felt her body slide slowly down that wall. She held her head in her hands. She heard voices calling out to her, she saw two nurses running toward her, but really only one. She was seeing double, and then she lost consciousness.

Again, there was activity in the hallway which quickly turned to ruckus. There was an emergency right outside of Bo's hospital room door, and Bo and Tia had no idea their conversation was overheard and led to a woman suffering a stroke.

"You are so angry," Tia said to him with tears in her eyes. Sure, she was scared for Mollie and what would happen if Bo defied her confidence. But, she was more terrified at the thought of her marriage crumbling. "You're not angry at me, or my friends, and their secrets certainly aren't an issue of importance here. What's important is you letting go of this anger you are harboring. You're upset and disappointed in yourself. You are not a weak man. You never thought you would succumb to addiction of any kind. You hurt your back, you popped a pain pill, and then that drug began to own you. It's time you own it." Tia surprised herself. She finally felt as if she understood.

Bo had tears welling up in his eyes now. She reached him. She finally reached him when she pinpointed exactly how he was feeling. He had failed himself, and that was the root of his evil. Failure had never before been an option. Not for him. Not for his wife. He now had to learn how to climb, one rung at a time, out of this sinkhole.

Tia slipped into the bed beside him and she held him. She may not have completely understood his addiction, but she now grasped that he could not overcome it alone.

CHAPTER 28

Blain and Mollie had arrived in the waiting room just minutes apart from each other. Brooke was telling them how Bo was admitted and Tia was with him when they suddenly heard the commotion coming from out in the hallway. Blain rose to his feet first, and the ladies followed him out. Brooke watched Blain start to run when he saw her. Even from thirty or forty feet away, he knew the woman down on the floor was his mother. Her shoulder length jet black hair, the same color Bryce had, caught his attention immediately.

***

Blain was sitting next to his mother's bedside. His father was now there, too. It was one day later, and after endless tests and scans, they had some answers.

The physician called it a hemorrhagic stroke, which in Julie Lanning's case was caused by uncontrolled high blood pressure. Her stress and worry over her missing son had gotten the best of her. Her health suffered gradually for more than a year. At only fifty-nine years old, she was facing a long road to recovery from partial paralysis on the right side of her body, and she could not speak. *It's possible she will make a full recovery*, the doctor had said. Whether or not Julie Lanning wanted to would be up to her.

High blood pressure made sense to all of them. Julie Lanning had been lost in worry and grief for a very long time. No one, however, had any idea what sent her reeling. She had finally learned the truth about her son. And, that revelation, happened in the most shocking, worst way.

***

Two and a half weeks later, Julie Lanning still had not spoken a word to her son, her husband, her therapists, or anyone on staff at the hospital where she still remained a patient. Her insurance would no longer support her hospital stay. She needed to be discharged to her home, or to a special care facility. On the last day of her hospital stay, Julie Lanning sat in the armchair beside her hospital bed. She had turned it to be able to see out of the window. A nurse had just left her, so she knew she would be alone for a while. She reached for the phone beside the bed with her left hand and dialed. She had no trouble getting out the words. She could speak, clearly and accurately. No one knew that, but her. When Detective Ty Clarke answered the phone after she had requested to speak with him, she told him who she was. He was happy to hear she was on the mend. He had heard otherwise, but believed it was a rumor now. She ceased the small talk, and told him exactly what he needed to know.

***

Eight hours later, Mollie was summoned into Ty Clarke's tiny office at the Breckenridge Police Department. She sat there with her hands, clammy to the point of ringing wet, on her lap. He kept her waiting, but finally arrived and shut the door behind him.

"Thank you for coming," he told her as she sat down behind his desk. Mollie remembered him from school, he was only one class ahead of her. Ty Clarke had done well for himself as a prominent member of the police force. He married after college and had twin boys who were the same age as Mollie's oldest son, Alex.

"You said it was urgent," Mollie responded, wondering what he knew. The secret had died with Freddy, and then Dee Campbell. Only her best friends knew, and they had all sworn each other to secrecy. *Maybe this was about something else*, Mollie thought, trying to calm herself. The detective seemed composed, so she tried to feed off of that.

"My wife, Cora and I met in college. She had just come out of a really bad relationship. She was broken." Mollie wondered where this was leading. She did not know his wife, or anything about her. She wasn't even entirely sure what she looked like, only having seen her maybe once or twice at school in the last few years since Alex started kindergarten. "Her ex-boyfriend had anger issues. He beat her." Detective Ty Clarke had sadness in his eyes, and Mollie reacted sincerely when she covered her hand over her mouth for a moment, before softly saying, *That's so awful, I'm sorry.*

"I never laid a hand on the man. I knew who he was. I could have used and abused my power to get that bastard in some way, shape, or form. But, I didn't. I just told myself that one day he would get what was coming to him." Mollie nodded her head. She, too, believed in karma. "Something was brought to my attention yesterday, and as an officer of the law, it's my job to address it. I called you here to ask you one question, Mollie." He paused, and Mollie continued to listen raptly. "Is Bryce Lanning's body buried in your backyard?" Julie Lanning had already told him Bryce was struck by a vehicle on the night of the blizzard a year and a half ago, and his body was secretly buried under the cemented swimming pool in the Sawyer's backyard. Freddy Sawyer was to blame for all of it. Had his wife or lover been an accomplice? At this point, Detective Ty Clarke did not specifically care.

Mollie sat there as her eyes widened and her face flushed. There was no other way. She had to tell the truth. She had children to raise, so maybe she would not be too severely punished. *Minimal jail time. Probation. Oh my God... she was about to pay for covering up Freddy's crime.* "Yes," she replied, honestly. And that was all she said. She could have defended herself. Begged for mercy for the sake of her children. But, she remained silent and scared, and he spoke again.

"The thought of that man under the ground, having been shown no respect after your husband's truck hit him, and eventually buried in the soil, under the rock and the cement, somehow feels like justice to me. Justice for my wife who was on the receiving end of his fists all those years ago. Justice for any other innocent woman he may have beaten. That son of a bitch can rot for the rest of forever for all I care. The secret you chose to keep will always be safe with me." When Detective Ty Clarke stopped speaking, Mollie was shocked and left speechless.

"I don't know what to say–" she began.

"Nothing is expected of you. You are not under arrest, you are not even here for questioning. I just wanted you to confirm the truth for me. It's time to take down the missing person flyers in this town. Bryce Lanning's case is now *unofficially* closed."

CHAPTER 29

It was early spring, and the weather was a mild forty-five degrees by nightfall. Breckenridge had received a light snowfall at noontime, which was typical there this time of year. The trees looked beautiful behind Brooke's cabin, all lightly dusted with glistening snow. On two pine trees, adjacent to each other, Blain had strung white lights as high as the eye could see. It looked beautiful and romantic as he stood there, glancing upward, and then beside him. A buddy of his since high school, whom he still played pool with at Ruby's, agreed to be his best man. Tia and Mollie and their children were there, too. It was a very small, intimate wedding.

Blain's mother could not be there. She still had not spoken a word and Bill Lanning had her placed in a facility where she could receive the care she needed. Care that he wasn't personally willing to provide for her. Blain invited her to his wedding. When he asked her if she wanted to come, she only shook her head no.

Bo was not present at the wedding either. He was halfway through his treatment at a drug rehab facility in Dillon. Tia and Mac had not been permitted to visit him yet, but soon they would be. They missed him, and they were incredibly proud of what he was doing. For himself, and for their family.

A sole trumpet in the woods played the wedding march and Blain's eyes were glistening as he watched his bride walk slowly and gracefully toward him. Brooke's wedding dress was stunning. It was custom made for her by a designer she knew from New York City. It was strapless, lacy, and she wore an organza wrap around her shoulders. The dress reached just above her ankles. Her figure was fuller as she had gained fifteen pounds and now fit into a curvy size six. Her dark hair was in an updo and she had large diamond hoop earrings hanging from her visible ear lobes. Blain stood there, never taking his eyes off of her. He looked dapper in his black dress pants, a black long-sleeved shirt with a solid white tie, and black patent tie dress shoes. They made a striking couple.

This wasn't their original plan. Flying off to Vegas no longer appealed to either of them. They only knew they did not want to wait to be united in marriage. Blain came up with the idea to say their vows in the woods behind the cabin. He told Brooke how that was the exact spot where he had completely and totally fallen in love with her. Her arms were wrapped around him then as he drove the snowmobile through the deep snow, weaving in and out between the trees. He specifically remembered looking up at those two pine trees. He saw the moon and the stars peeking through them, and that was the moment he knew he would do anything for her. She made him feel as if he could rope the moon and wish upon any star and inevitably have her love him back as much as he loved her.

Blain's idea to get married out there was a delightful surprise to Brooke. She treasured the idea. When they were pronounced husband and wife, Brooke knew for certain this was only the beginning of a good life together. But, it was not only going to be just the two of them for very long, as she was already eight weeks pregnant.

ABOUT THE AUTHOR

Uncertainty. We've all been in that state of mind. Some of us live that way all of the time. Worry and stress over things we cannot control, cannot change, often leave us with doubts and fears that could drive us to the brink. If we allow it.

I was inspired to write about uncertainty in a way that involved creating a character (Brooke) who was trying to deal with losing a man she loved and not knowing what happened to him. I wanted to address open-ended loss, which is unlike any kind of grief because it doesn't resolve itself.

Little did I know that before this book would be published, I would find myself in the midst of grief. The emotions of grief are so raw, so revealing, and so consuming. You never know when it's going to hit you. A memory. A song triggering a special moment. Just being somewhere you used to be with someone, and now they are no longer there. You dwell. You over think. You cry. You feel angry and disappointed that this is how it ends. It's a whirlwind like I've never experienced before. There's absolutely nothing you can do when someone you love is just gone. And you wonder when, or if, the pain will subside. When I lost a very dear friend to an untimely death, just weeks ago, I forced myself to re-read my own words in this story. *Missing You* healed me, or at least put me on a path of healing. While the story is entirely fiction, my own words helped me to see that life is for the living. Those we loved and lost are okay. We will see them again one day, but for now we have to live. The world does not stop for us. And the last thing I know my dear friend would have wanted was for any of her family and friends to lose themselves in grief.

In this book, I intended to create a character who didn't know whether to grieve, to move on, or to hang on to hope. The character, in so many ways, did give up on how to live. She was in limbo with no certainty of ever being freed from the waiting and wondering. She was clinging to both hope and suffering. And then she found a way to live again.

The circumstances behind living with uncertainty can vary. We don't have to experience tragedy to know what it feels like to feel consumed with thoughts which could easily make us dial crazy. The key is to seize the good things. Hold tight to memories and the moments that make us happy, and just live.

This is my seventh novel. Inspiration continues to strike me in many different ways. In this case, I heard a song recorded by country music artist, Alan Jackson. The song, titled, "The One You're Waiting On" instantly painted a picture for me as the storyline for *Missing You* unfolded in my mind.

It's distressing to see people allowing life to pass by, while so many chances are left untaken. Whatever your situation is, seize your chance! You may never get another one.

As always, thank you for reading!

love,
Lori Bell